The Truth About Benjamin Franklin

A Novel

The Truth About Benjamin Franklin

A novel by

Joyce G. Snyder

Writers Club Press
San Jose New York Lincoln Shanghai

The Truth About
Benjamin Franklin
A Novel

Writers Club Press
an imprint of iUniverse.com, Inc.

For information address:
iUniverse.com, Inc.
5220 S 16th, Ste. 200
Lincoln, NE 68512
www.iuniverse.com

ISBN: 0-595-17865-0

Printed in the United States of America

To my daughters, Heather Wagner and Gabrielle Wagner-Mann, for their love and support; and in memory of my mother, Dorothy Snyder....all very special women.

And always, to Z, for his love, guidance and inspiration.

Acknowledgements

Many thanks to my friends and family who gave me encouragement and support in following my dream: Jerry Wasielewski, my good friend and sounding board; Paul Wilson, for all the 'walkin and the talkin'; Harold and Nikki Huggins, for the many good chats and insights; Caroline Wachsberger, for helping me 'interpret;' Sue Nielsen, for all the 'breaks'; Anne Harrigan, Judy Toll, Brian Walls, Ginny Murray, Kathy Smith, Eileen Murphy, Elen Maletich, Sharon Faith, Rich & Eileen Clauser, Jack & Irene Sonatore, Suzanne Lagay and Dolly Taschner for believing I could do it.

I love you all!

Chapter 1

Carol Byrd stuffed papers into her briefcase in anticipation of working on her book over the weekend. John would be away at the MLA meeting and that left a gloriously empty house and the freedom to do what she really wanted to do, uninterrupted. She looked at the stack of ungraded papers on her desk and reluctantly put those in her briefcase too. Having to choose between Ben Franklin and grading student papers was not a tough choice, she thought wryly.

She saw at the last minute a fat manila envelope on the far corner of her cluttered desk and recognized her graduate assistant's handwriting on the outside. "More BF stuff," he wrote in a black felt tip pen. She opened it and saw photocopies of text, two inches thick. The first title caught her eye, "Ben Franklin's Mojo." She shook her head in disgust at how slang had invaded even scholarly journals. She put the envelope, along with the other Franklin papers, in her already bulging briefcase. On her way out she scooped up two books, thinking at the last minute she might need them, turned the light switch off with her elbow and was out the door.

Friday afternoon at four-thirty, campus was nearly deserted; students had long since left for their weekend activities. Carol walked the short distance to the faculty parking lot and emptied her armload into the back seat of her car. As she drove through the campus, she noticed with appreciation the beauty of the grounds and the buildings, and felt a moment of contentment. The campus in repose, as she liked to think of it, always gave her that feeling. Pretty as a picture in a college catalog, a few students strolling on the tree-lined paths, it always symbolized for her this academic life she'd chosen...the ivory tower, the joy of intellectual pursuits.

Numen was a college town in the Midwest. Bodley University was the only reason the town maintained a population of almost 50,000; it being the main source of employment as well as of most cultural events. It had two movie theaters, two hospitals and the usual disproportionate number of bars and fast food restaurants; but also in disproportion, it had a full symphony orchestra, three art museums, and an active performing theater. Plays, written and acted by local artists, dance recitals and concerts were performed regularly. A poetry reading with several hundred in attendance was not uncommon on any given night in Numen. It was a town that cherished its cultural sufficiency and its ethnic diversity. Education and artistic culture were almost community ideals in Numen.

Carol Byrd was a professor in the Women's Studies Department, with a background in language and literature. Before the Women's Studies Department was formed, Carol taught linguistics, semantics and history of the English language, but her feminist leanings produced papers with a definite feminist criticality to them. She briefly chaired the Women's Studies department, but when the opportunity came to return to full-time teaching and research, she took it, preferring that to administrative work.

Her husband, John Byrd was a professor of English. Now in their early forties, they'd long ago decided that children were not for them; that any needs they may have for reproducing and nurturing would be met by scholarly writing and maybe a pet or two.

They lived in an old Victorian house that must have been gracious in its original state, and over the years they worked on it, painstakingly restoring the oak woodwork and modernizing it just enough for their comfort. The result was a functional blend of charm and convenience. The house was on a large, tree-filled lot with a small pond in the back under a weeping willow. They cleared one corner of their property for gardening, and each spring planted vegetables and flowers, sharing the gardening work. John preferred tending to the rose bushes and flowerbeds, while Carol, being more practical, liked the yield of actual food for all the work they did.

As she pulled into her driveway she saw her husband's car already there and felt a slight disappointment, then quickly chided herself. It wasn't that she wasn't glad to see him. No, it was just that she liked coming home to an empty house. She smiled as she thought how that would sound if said out loud. *I like coming home to an empty house.* The quiet and stillness of an empty house was soothing after spending the day in the outside world of noise and chatter. She always dropped her briefcase in her study first, then walked from room to room reveling in the quiet and the order, becoming calm herself in the stillness of the house. Her consciousness impressed itself on the silence and that created a kind of kinship between her and the house. At least this is the way she saw it. She tried to explain this once to her husband, who said he understood, but she could tell by the tolerant, bemused smile that this, like other of her quirks, mystified him.

When he arrived home first, she knew she'd have to start talking, a continuation of a day of talking. She wanted to talk with him, just not the same moment she walked in the door.

She went immediately to her study to deposit her briefcase and books. John's study was at the other end of the hall and the room in between was the library, which had adjoining doors to both rooms. Between them they had almost five thousand books, so they converted this huge center room to a library. Carpenters built floor-to-ceiling shelves on all four walls. They added track lighting, comfortable chairs, a couch and a writing table. This room, devoted to reading, symbolized their life style: quiet, comfortable and intellectual.

She went into the kitchen where she heard John preparing dinner.

"Hi, honey."

He looked up from the chicken he was washing at the sink and leaned to her for a kiss. "Hi, welcome home. I'm making chicken in orange sauce for dinner, OK?"

"Fine, your specialty" she smiled, giving him a quick kiss as she touched him briefly on the back. "How did the orals go?" She opened the refrigerator and pulled out ingredients for a salad.

"He passed. Not as strong in American as European, but we decided to give him a pass." John was on the orals committee for a Ph.D. candidate, one of his duties as a graduate professor.

He basted the cut-up chicken with orange juice and butter and put it in the glass baking dish, carefully placing it in the oven as he related some anecdotes from his day.

"How was your day?"

She shrugged as she began cutting a boiled potato, radishes and celery into a bowl.

"OK. I had a conference with that ball-busting student I told you about. He accused me of giving him a lower grade because he was the only man in the class."

"And you told him, of course, that it was really because he writes and thinks like a third-grader?"

She smiled. "No, dear, I was a little more tactful than that. I told him he wrote like a high school freshman. Hand me the olive oil, will you?"

"Oh, that's much more tactful." He turned and rummaged in the cabinet and handed her the bottle. He also got out plates and held them, looking at her quizzically. "Patio?"

"Oh, do you think it's warm enough outside? That would be nice. By the way, what time are you leaving tomorrow?"

"Renee Frazer is picking me up at five. The meeting starts at nine. It should take about three hours to get to Chicago, but we're allowing time for a breakfast stop."

"What's the agenda?"

"Style sheet changes, for one. Can you believe a room full of intelligent adults is going to spend hours debating such things as comma placements?"

"Oh, John, you know you're exaggerating."

"Not by much. Would you like a glass of wine?"

"Yes, please."

It was early spring and though the days had been warm, it cooled off quickly when the sun went down. He gathered napkins and utensils and went outside to set the patio table. She sprinkled the vegetables with the oil and set it on the counter. She looked out at John carefully arranging the things on the patio table. His lean frame bent over the table as though concentrating on an intricate problem. At forty-five his brown hair was streaked with grey, but in his sweatshirt and jeans he looked youthful and physically fit. He looked up and saw her watching him through the patio door. She smiled slowly, unaware that this transformed her from pretty to beautiful in John's eyes. Her hazel eyes were gazing steadily at him. Her short blond hair was wavy and one lock of her hair fell over her forehead. He watched as she unconsciously pushed it back. He responded with a wave, not realizing that though he was the recipient of the smile, he was not the cause.

Her eyes, though apparently focused on John, were not really seeing him. Her vision was turned inward to the subject of her book, and she was having an inner dialogue with him that brought the smile. John came back in and stood smiling in front of her, causing her to refocus her attention to him. Carol wasn't always generous with those warm, inviting smiles and John was grateful to see the affection on her face.

After dinner, they cleaned up the kitchen together and went for a walk around their neighborhood, chatting companionably, arms swinging at their sides. Later, Carol wanted to go to her study and write down the earlier conversation with Ben before she forgot, but John had to go to bed early and he clearly wanted her to go with him. After they made love, she thought she'd go downstairs and work, but John's arm was heavy across her middle and she didn't want to wake him. His alarm was set for 4:30 a.m. and he needed his sleep. She settled under the covers comfortably and thought of how she'd have the whole day tomorrow to work on the book. Turning her thoughts to the 18th century, she gradually drifted off to sleep.

Chapter 2

Carol got up shortly after John left, not wanting to waste a minute of her day alone. She put on a sweat suit and socks and went downstairs. She made a pot of coffee which John apparently didn't take the time to do. It was just as well. She liked it freshly perked and prepared her way. She carefully spooned half decaf and half regular coffee into the basket, then sprinkled it with cinnamon, a little vanilla for flavor and a dash of salt to cut the acid. As the coffee maker started its noises, she turned the dishwasher on. They loaded it last night but forgot to run it.

She opened the sliding glass door to the redwood deck and stepped out. She loved being outdoors at dawn, the night darkness still hovering, the birds just beginning to wake and sing. She scooped birdseed from the twenty-pound bag by the door and filled the bird feeders and the bowl she kept on the ground for chipmunks and squirrels. The chirping birds were the only sounds on this spring morning. She went back in and filled a mug with coffee and came out to watch the slowly lightening sky. She sat on a wood bench against the house and pulled her knees up to her chin, holding her coffee mug close for warmth.

She always liked this time alone when the world was quiet and her own mind hadn't yet shifted into high gear, ordering and arranging her day. Breathing deeply in the cool morning air she was glad for the warmth of the sweat suit. With her stillness, the birds eventually began coming for the feed, accepting her presence as part of their landscape.

She watched the smaller birds dip their tiny heads for the seed and then scatter at the least disturbance. The early bird gets the worm she said softly, chuckling to herself. Blue jays came... always a visual treat for Carol...and she observed that despite their loud chatter, they were more skittish than other birds and were the first to fly off at any disturbance. With their loud squawking, they put up a good front of being brave, but Carol decided it was all show; they were really rather cowardly. She liked them anyway.

Once when a jay had been the only bird there, Carol spoke softly to him, telling him how beautiful he was and how much she liked him. The bird, ever cautious, flew from branch to branch watching her, but apparently listening. Then, to Carol's surprise, he warbled in a melodious voice, unlike she'd ever heard a jay do before. Gone was the furious squawking and for a few moments his beautiful melody filled her with awe and love.

Today she saw crows hovering nearby waiting for their chance at the seed. Carol liked crows too, their sleek black coats, their air of something primal, mysterious. She usually put more substantial food out for the crows: chicken or turkey carcasses, table food scraps...they ate it all. She knew Ted Hughes was right about crows. She thought of his poems about them, and how he endowed the crow with a kind of mystical, cynical wisdom.

She wrapped her hands around the mug and feeling the serenity brought by this morning contact with nature, went inside.

She refilled her coffee mug and went to her study. She opened the blinds to let the morning light in and to give her the view of the trees in her side yard. Still barely six o'clock, she turned on her desk lamp until the sun would flood the room and provide enough light.

She turned on the computer and brought up the file she was working on. So far, she hadn't shown what she'd written to anyone, not even John, but she knew that soon that would have to change. She was going to have to get some feedback on this project, and on what she'd written so far. She was sure enough about what she was doing not to be intimidated by negative criticism, but she also knew there was a chance the publisher would not accept this manuscript as it was being written. It wasn't exactly what they had contracted for. She took a sip of her coffee and read from the computer screen.

Benjamin Franklin was born January 17, 1706 in Boston, to Josiah and Abiah Folger Franklin. He was the youngest son of Josiah's seventeen children; ten by his second wife Abiah. Josiah was a chandler and, as tradition dictated, he dedicated his youngest son, Ben to the church, then changed his mind and wanted him to take up the candle-making trade.

Wax and tallow did not interest young Ben who wanted to go to sea. An older brother had run away to sea and was thought lost for many years; therefore the father was not going to allow this to happen twice. His father exposed his young son to several trades, hoping he would find something he liked, but Ben had a fondness for poetry, the sea, and books, and couldn't settle on a trade. Eventually his father placed him as an apprentice with his older brother, James, a printer, and Ben found he liked the printing press and working with words and ink.

He did not, however, get along with his older brother and as soon as he had the opportunity, he left his apprenticeship, and, rebelling against the strictures of family, ran away to Philadelphia, penniless and just sixteen-years old.

He found a job in a print shop and worked for Samuel Keimer, who, like Ben's brother, was a cruel master. On the promise of financing for his own print shop, Franklin went to England to buy a press, and spent the next two years in London, "sowing his wild oats" shall we say?

In 1726 he returned to Philadelphia, set up a print shop with borrowed funds and in 1730 married Deborah Read, whom he had courted before he went to England. By this time he also had an illegitimate son, William, whom Deborah (though not the mother) agreed to raise. The identity of William's mother has never been known.

At age twenty-four he had his own printing press, his own newspaper and his own general store where he and Debbie worked side by side.

In 1732 he launched Poor Richard's Almanac which became an overnight success, eventually extending to a readership of 10,000.

His son, Francis, was born that year and four years later, in 1736, died of smallpox, a grief Franklin carried always.

In 1737 he was made Postmaster of Philadelphia, and this began a period of public service that lasted essentially, the rest of his life. In 1739 he invented the Pennsylvania furnace (later called the Franklin stove). In 1743 his daughter, Sally was born. In 1748 he retired at age forty-two from his store and print shop and began another life, first as a scientist with electrical experiments, then as emissary of the colonies.

In 1753 he became postmaster general of all the colonies and in 1757 went to England as ambassador to attempt conciliatory changes and agreements with the crown. The principal issue was taxation. He stayed in England this time for five years, returning to Philadelphia in 1762. He went again to England in 1764 and was not to come home for eleven years. His wife, who feared crossing the ocean, was not with him.

In December, 1774, his wife, Deborah died. They had been married forty-four years, fifteen of the last eighteen spent apart. He returned to Philadelphia in 1775 to help draft the Declaration of Independence, and he presided at the Pennsylvania Constitutional Convention.

In 1776 he sailed for France to attempt to commission France's aid in the colonies' war with England. Eminently successful in France he arranged the French alliance, negotiated and signed the Treaty of Paris and remained there for the next nine years.

In 1784 he wrote the second part of his **Autobiography** *and in 1785 returned to Philadelphia where he was elected President of Pennsylvania. In 1787 he was a delegate to the Constitutional Convention, and in 1788, he (at long last) retired from public life. In 1789 he finished writing the last section of his* **Autobiography***.*

He died April 17, 1790, having been ill for a few years with kidney stones and gout.

These are the basic facts of Benjamin Franklin's life. Packed into those eighty-four years and three months were several careers in many fields: inventor, writer, printer, editor, statesman, tradesman, postmaster, plenipotentiary, ambassador, diplomat, scientist...and that list is probably not complete. He was a versatile man, a genius of a man.

He is known, not only for his scientific and political accomplishments, but also for his personality. His sense of humor is legendary, as is his honesty, his moral disposition, his pragmatism and frugality. These character traits are practically synonymous with his name. Also well known and of interest to many historians, is his fondness for women. This is interpreted variously as licentiousness, lecherousness, debauchery and more simply, as an appreciation for women. How accurate are these judgments, rendered by history who in turn received them from his peers, many of whom were moralists and Puritans (and maybe jealous of his success with the fair sex)?

Does a fondness for women unequivocally imply that he was lascivious, promiscuous? That lust was his main interest in the female form?

Depending on which historian you read, this is the judgment concluded on Ben Franklin's female relationships. Is it unfair? Yes, I think so. But a more important question that scholars and historians should ask is, Is it accurate?

Carol turned from her computer and lifted her head slightly as though listening. The soft ticking of a clock was the only sound in the room. She noticed that sunlight was on her desk, so she reached up and turned off the desk lamp.

She put her hands on the keyboard and waited, half hoping, half fearing that she'd feel that tingling of her skin that announced his presence. Nothing. She looked at what she'd written from an editing point of view and began working on it.

He'd told her he wouldn't often come the way he had before. She couldn't expect that. He told her to just write. She'd know.

Chapter 3

By the time John got home the light had faded and she again turned on the desk lamp. With food and stretch breaks, Carol had been at it all day. She looked at the clock when she heard John's car pull in the driveway and saw with surprise that it was nearly eight o'clock. She stood up, reaching her hands to the ceiling, then bent over, letting her muscles relax and her body droop forward, touching her hands to the floor. This quick hathayoga hanging position always refreshed her.

She went to the foyer and flipped on the light just as John opened the door.

"Ah, light as if by magic. Hello."

"Hi," she said kissing him and hugging him close for a moment. "How'd it go?"

"Scintillating, stimulating, enervating."

"Uh-oh, one of those words doesn't belong," she smiled. "You look tired."

"It was a long day and all those hours in the car with Renee Frazer just exacerbated my ennui."

She laughed. "Whew. I can tell you've been with the MLA crew today...all those big words," she mocked him. She walked into the kitchen and he followed, taking his jacket off and draping it on a chair as he passed.

"What's this, no dinner ready?" He looked at the empty counters and table in dismay. "I was dreaming of something delicious and ready."

"Sorry, dear. I was writing all day and didn't think to do that. Besides, I didn't know when you'd be home."

"That's OK. Actually Renee and I stopped at a diner and I had a salad. Figured that would be my appetizer for the gourmet feast you would prepare."

"Boy were you wrong," she said opening the refrigerator and poking at the various containers. "But you know, I can have a casserole together in minutes. I have leftover chicken, leftover beans, cook a little pasta, throw in a little sauce, add a little cheese. Whaddya say?"

"Sure, sounds good. Will it go with what I'm drinking?"

"Which is?"

"I don't know, what do we have?" He stood next to her at the refrigerator and reached in for a bottle of wine that had been opened and recapped. "Ah, this."

"Good choice, sir. Pour one for me too while you're at it."

He handed her a wine glass and she took a sip as she began assembling the ingredients and putting a pot of water on the stove.

"How'd your writing go today?"

She looked into the casserole bowl as she answered.

"Pretty good. I'm trying to organize my notes...you know order the different topics."

"When will I get to see some of this? You've been working on it long enough to have something written."

"Oh, soon. It's still very rough."

"Do you know where you're going with it?"

"What do you mean?"

He took a sip of his wine and picked up a cold green bean with his fingers. "You know, you were going to skewer Dr. Franklin for being...what? too sexy? too moral? not moral enough? You haven't told me what your thesis is. Don't you know yet?"

"Well, I do, but..."

"But what? Is there a problem?"

She was unsure how to tell John about how different her focus was from what she'd originally discussed with him. It was too weird, she thought, to just mention it casually. She needed more time on the subject.

"It's not turning out the way I thought," she said evasively. "I mean, my research is leading me in a kind of a different direction."

"What's different?"

"Well, I think I may not be writing what the editor wants. In fact, I think it may be contrary to what they have in mind."

John pretended to be shocked, "Oh no, do you mean, could it be, is there a chance you will not demolish Dr. Franklin?"

She smiled at him. "Perhaps. Would that shock you?"

He finished his glass of wine and put an arm around her, kissing her on the temple. "Honey, whatever you write will be brilliant. And if it shocks, so what? I know you're a good researcher, so if you're doing your home-work, you'll back up everything you say. Right?"

"Suppose I can't, you know, back it up in conventional ways. What do you think?"

"Do you mean you're going to *speculate?*" He said it as though it was a dirty word.

She laughed at his tone. "No, not really. But suppose I say something I know to be true, but can't validate with any historical record?"

"How could you know it to be true if it isn't verifiable in any histo-ry book?"

"You know," she said, a little embarrassed, putting the pasta into the boiling water, "the way I validate other truths...within."

"You're joking? Do you really think a premise will be accepted because you say, 'I have this strong intuitive feeling that this is so?' Surely, you jest, my dear."

"Well, I would be a little more descriptive, but in essence, yes, I'd have to explain an alternative method of arriving at fact and truth."

"Truth, maybe, in your eyes. But fact can only be validated in the tra-ditional way: researching historical sources."

"Then I guess I have a dilemma," she smiled at him, not looking concerned. "Do you want to shower before we eat?"

"Yes, but I want to hear more about this 'dilemma.' Just how different is your approach?"

"I'm warning you...it might be real different."

"Well, different can be good," he said carefully. He watched her as she mixed the leftovers in an oven-going glass bowl and marveled at how creative she could be with food, as well as in other areas of her life. He waited for her to explain further, but she was concentrating on food and seemed to think the topic was done.

"The pasta's cooking," she said. "You have about ten minutes. OK?"

He hesitated a moment, then went upstairs to take a shower. She finished preparing the casserole, setting it into the hot oven to heat. "I wonder how good this different will be," she mused out loud.

Chapter 4

Though Carol's field was originally linguistics, by the time she was writing her dissertation in 1973, the women's movement was in full swing and she was spiritually and intellectually a part of it. She had begun an informal study, in those early years of the women's movement, of the way history and literature had discriminated against women through language. Her observation powers were keen and she read with a fine discrimination, noticing nuances as well as blatant examples. She wrote her dissertation on this subject ("Gender Bias in Historical and Literary Language") and though there certainly was not much literature on that topic, she wrote bravely, breaking new ground.

Initially, she taught basic linguistics and semantics, but as feminist courses were added to the curriculum, Carol was the obvious person to teach them. Within five years, she went from assistant to associate professor, based on her reputation and her increasing list of publications. In 1981, a Women's Studies department was formed and Carol was asked to chair it.

She was instrumental in bringing prominent women to the college to guest lecture, and the young undergraduate women began responding with enthusiasm to the new major. She often arranged for key people in the women's movement to speak at her college: Gloria Steinem, Betty Friedan and other well-known feminists in other fields. She herself was popular as a lecturer on the subjects of language and feminism and was often invited to other colleges to speak. The department became strong and prestigious under her direction and after six years, she turned over the chair and returned to teaching, writing, and research. Free of the administrative duties that had prevented a lot of her research, she was delighted and relieved with the change.

Thus, in late 1987 when she was contacted by a publisher to write a book on the founding fathers, with a feminist slant, she agreed. It had to be fair, they emphasized, but the focus had to be on the sexism, discrimination, and attitudes of the founding fathers toward women, making the connection that the principles on which our country was founded were influenced by the inherent sexism of early American men. The project was still formative and her input was welcome. She could edit a set of monographs as well as writing one herself, or she could just write a book

Carol accepted the assignment, choosing Benjamin Franklin for what she felt at the time, no apparent reason. Madison, Washington, Adams, and Jefferson were assigned to other writers. She knew little about Franklin, but his reputation as a ladies' man was well known, so she thought his character would yield the most fertile, feminist copy.

At forty-one, she had reached the rank of full professor, and publishing projects like this were icing on the cake. Carol assigned her graduate assistant, Jake, to begin the research.

"Let's look at everything written on Franklin and women. That'll probably keep us for awhile. I'll also want what's written on the subject of sexism and the founding fathers, and of course, check out the others for what's written about them on that topic."

"But mostly Franklin?"

"Yes, he's my man," she said with a grin.

"He's got a reputation as a lecher, doesn't he?"

"More or less, though that might be rather strong. Let's survey the literature and see how history has treated him. I really don't know. He's not someone I'd normally read about. My knowledge of the American Revolution is somewhat limited."

Jake delivered after two days, a stack of books and a list of articles.

"Check which ones you want and I'll get them," he said.

"Good God, there's a lot. Who would have thought there'd be so much interest in an old, dead lecher?" She scanned the bibliography, but it was lengthy.

"I'll do this tonight and give it to you tomorrow. What are those books?"

"Basic biography mostly. There's more, but I figured six was enough to start with. Do you want me to work with those?"

She hesitated. Normally this would be a task he could easily do for her. Read the index and make notes of anything connected with her topic and/or photocopy the pages.

"I'm not quite sure what I'm looking for. I mean, yes the obvious, but I have to know more about the man...not just this one area. Let me take them, I'll do it myself. You start on the other founding fathers...not as extensively, just what you can find on their attitudes toward women. Do you like this project?" she asked with a grin.

"Well, it's not exactly linguistics, Professor Byrd, if you know what I mean," he said dryly.

She laughed. "Oh, stop complaining. This is much more valuable to your education. Just think, Jake, you'll be the only male professor of linguistics who knows just as much about feminism in history. That's a broad education."

"Yeah, yeah. Gotta go, I have a class. See you later, Carol." He left and Carol picked up one of the books.

Jake was twenty-three and working on his master's degree in linguistics. Last semester when Carol had an opening for a graduate assistant, her previous one having graduated and moved on, Jake applied for the job. She was surprised to see a male applicant. Traditionally only women applied to work for her, so Carol was intrigued. She interviewed him and found him not only intelligent and with traits that promised reliability, but he had a sincere interest in understanding what was happening between men and women at this time in history. His bent was toward psycho-linguistics, but he had a girlfriend who was a staunch feminist and since he loved her, he wanted to understand her. He felt working for Carol would be a plus for him, not only because of her reputation in the field of linguistics, but also in feminist criticism. He was hoping to learn a lot from her.

Carol was glad for the change. There was a period of time in the women's movement, she recalled, when feminists felt it was necessary to profess to be anti-men, and a lot of the students came to the program with this inclination. Carol's take on the women's movement was more intellectual than emotional. Change had to come about but it had to be because of cooperation between the sexes, she believed, not contempt between them. The change, she believed, would benefit both sexes, freeing them from rules and jails that imprisoned them both.

Still, a certain amount of resentment and anger was understandable. Oppressed in so many ways for so long, women were fighting not only for equality, but also for very basic freedoms. Carol understood that the period of upset that engendered hatred and anger was part of any change movement. She believed it had either to pass into a more modified and acceptable emotion or it would solidify into war.

She thought having a male assistant might help the image as well as the cause. She was the most visible feminist in the college, so she thought that would be a good example of tolerance and cooperation.

She glanced at her appointment book; none until three o'clock. She put her feet up on her desk and started reading about Benjamin Franklin, making notes on a legal pad as she read.

Chapter 5

Her initial impression of her very cursory survey was that Franklin biographers either loved him or hated him. Their books praised him or condemned him. Carol thought this interesting that he evoked such strong and opposite feelings. Where was scholarly objectivity?

Before she started reading she wrote a page of her own pre-research impressions of Franklin. What did she know of him? She found her knowledge was superficial...probably what most Americans knew: he was one of the founding fathers, he invented stuff, he signed the Declaration of Independence and he liked women. A lot of the folk wisdom captured in pithy little proverbs was credited to him.

Carol was embarrassed at how little she knew. His face was of course familiar, but his personal history was nothing to her. She vaguely remembered reading his *Autobiography* for an undergraduate American literature course and being unimpressed with his droll style. Still, that was her starting point. The Carl Van Doren biography seemed to be the standard, published in 1938, so she started there. Van Doren was admiring, that much was evident in the first few pages and his research appeared to be thorough, methodical and fairly objective; the book a chronological record of Franklin's life. She quickly became bored.

"Why am I wasting my time on this project?" she asked herself. "I have no axe to grind with Franklin, why am I looking for ways to crucify him on the altar of the women's movement?"

Her enthusiasm for the project waned as she began the actual work. The truth was, she admitted after a few days, her heart wasn't in it. She would complete the project, but she knew from experience that unless her heart was really into doing something, it would not be a great success.

She discussed it with John.

"I signed a contract for the book, and I have a year to deliver, but the thought of spending that much time in the 18th century is depressing."

"Can you change the approach to make it of interest to you?"

"I don't know…a book about Franklin is still a book about Franklin. I think I made a mistake taking this on."

"Can you get out of the contract?" This was the point in discussion when Carol got frustrated with him. She didn't want him to come up with the solution for her, especially not so quickly. She didn't want to leap to the end conclusion, rather walk through all the arguments between here and there to see if there was a different solution. She wanted to keep talking it out until the solution appeared to her.

"It's not that," she said impatiently. "Of *course* I can always get out of the contract. I'm just not sure what I should do."

John watched her, her frown indicating deep thought.

"Maybe if you just keep reading, something will click. You haven't come across anything of interest?"

"No, not really. I kept thinking all the reading would yield an idea, but nothing yet. The women thing is what I feel I have to focus on, but I don't know if the substance is there for a book…it's sort of been done. I don't want to touch the political and I don't know enough about science to do his inventions. Any of those angles could work."

"He was such a large man, spiritually speaking, maybe…"

She cut him off, "What do you mean spiritually?"

"Well, I meant, he was into so many things, so many interests, he was so…I don't know…integrated. He was a thinking man, obviously."

"One of the things he's accused of is being non-religious, not concerned with the spiritual. Do you think otherwise?"

John let the newspaper down and gestured with his free hand, "I just mean other than his physical accomplishments, he was truly a man of substance. He couldn't accomplish all that he did without deep thinking, pondering, contemplation. To me, that's spiritual. Yes no?" he asked as she stayed silent, looking thoughtful.

"Maybe looking below the surface of him might yield something." John looked apologetic. "I'm sorry I'm not very helpful here."

"No, you just gave me an idea. By the way, how do you know so much about Franklin?"

"I really don't know all that much. When I was teen-ager I got fascinated with him for some reason. I read a biography and then I think the fascination eventually passed."

"Thanks." She jumped up from the chair, and dashed out of the room.

"You're welcome," John said after her, smiling and shaking his head.

        *   *   *

In her study she picked up the Van Doren book and started reading again. The man behind the man, she mused.

The dreams started that night.

Franklin came into the room leaning on a cane and greeted George Washington and his aide heartily. Despite his frailty, he exuded good will and humor. He was three years away from his death, and though his hair was thinned and gray, his eyes still had a twinkle and his smile was warm as he greeted his old friend. They were dining together at Franklin's house in Philadelphia. A middle-aged woman served the meal with an air of both pride and humility.

"Thank you my dear, Sally," he said to his daughter.

Washington spoke very little but listened, charmed and amused by Franklin's witty monologue. He spoke with a lightness and a gentle teasing manner entertaining his guests with his amusing conversation. A voice said, "May 14, 1787."

Carol sat bolt upright in bed, wide awake with this dream. She went downstairs to her study to flip through some preliminary Franklin notes and his relationship with George Washington. She discovered that the constitutional convention met in May of 1787 in Philadelphia. It shouldn't be too hard to ascertain if he dined with Washington on that date, she thought. But she knew with a sudden clarity that though the date could possibly be confirmed, the conversation most surely could not.

She sat in her study at three in the morning, wondering if she *actually* had eavesdropped on a conversation between the first president and Franklin. And if this were so, she thought with a smile, she was possibly the only one in the world who knew what words were spoken during that dinner. She quickly recorded the dream as accurately as she could. As she finished writing and was about to go back to bed, it occurred to her that she hardly gave Washington a glance as she witnessed the scene. He never held much interest for her as an historical personality; she thought him dull. Her attraction had definitely been to Franklin.

Perhaps a week or so after that, when her Franklin interest was re-stimulated, she had another dream.

In this one he was standing behind Marie Antoinette as she sat at a type of boudoir table. She may have been primping and Franklin was being outrageously flattering. She clearly basked in it.

Carol watched this scene, as she had watched the earlier one with Washington, as a detached observer. She made a note that Franklin seemed taller than his pictures depicted him, less of a paunch and his nostrils had more flair than paintings gave him. She found herself being utterly charmed by this scene. Though she later confirmed that Franklin had indeed visited the court of Louis XVI, nowhere did she find that he had any kind of intimacy with Marie Antoinette as the scene she witnessed implied.

The dream that changed the direction of her book was the third one when he appeared to her with an almost tangible presence. Rather than observing him from an invisible standpoint as she had in the other two, in this one he addressed her directly.

She was sleeping soundly, spoon fashion against John's back when she heard someone call her name. A light sleeper, she opened her eyes and listened. John was snoring softly and she heard the sound of the wind through the open window. Otherwise it was silent. She waited a moment and was about to close her eyes when she saw a flash of light near the bed and suddenly she was in a vacuum of silence, hearing nothing, not even John's breathing. She found herself sitting up and in the midst of the light stood the image of Benjamin Franklin.

He held out his left hand in an inviting gesture and he was smiling. Wordlessly she got up and followed him through the doorway. They entered a room and he closed the door behind them.

"We don't want to wake John," he said with a chuckle.

"Where did this room come from?" Carol looked about in wonder. They walked right through the bedroom wall but instead of being outside in mid-air they were standing in what appeared to be a conference room with a table and two chairs. Papers and books were spread on the table. Carol realized she hadn't put a robe on; she slept in the nude and was suddenly embarrassed. She looked down at herself and saw only light, the same hazy white light that Franklin stood in. "This is lucid dreaming," a voice inside her head seemed to say and she thought, "Ah," as though that explained everything.

"Please, sit down," he indicated one of the chairs. She did so and her attention was immediately drawn to the papers spread out on the table.

"This is my book," she looked at him surprised, not knowing how she knew this. "But I haven't even started it yet."

"It's quite in progress here," he said enjoying her surprise. "You see, before anything can be manifested in the physical world, it first has to be born here and in fact, have a reality here."

"Where is here?"

"Why, where you are," he smiled spreading his arms out to encompass the room and the bedroom and all the space around them. "But no matter, I want to discuss your book with you. Finding your direction seems to be presenting you with a problem?"

"Yes, it is." Carol picked up one of the pages of manuscript and tried to read, but it was in hieroglyphics, impossible to decipher.

"There are certain images of me that have become part of my own personal history and they are, for the most part, erroneous images. It is this I'd like you to correct."

One part of her mind was recording this, observing his physical characteristics. His clear, hazel eyes had a firm seriousness that was relieved of being stern by the glint of humor. He looked to be in his fifties. All of these observations were instantaneous and almost unconscious.

"How?"

"In your book. I will guide the writing so that you don't make the same mistakes others have in writing about me."

"I don't understand. Why me?"

He smiled faintly and looked intently at her, his hazel eyes piercing and unblinking. He seemed to be assessing something inwardly. Finally his eyes relaxed and he said simply, "You were chosen. Now, shall we get to work?" He indicated the papers.

"How will I know what to write?" She wanted to argue but he was already motioning for her to pick up the pen.

"My dear Carol," he said affectionately and this tone both perplexed and warmed her. "Trust that as you sit at your computer…a fine invention by the way…the words will come to you as easily as rain comes to a spring day."

Carol turned her head and suddenly she was awake in her bed, her face brushing John's arm as he turned over in his sleep.

She sat up again and looked toward the wall where the room had been. There was only the window and it was closed. She looked at her body and it was flesh.

She glanced at the clock; it was three a.m.

"Weird," she said to herself, wanting to turn over and go back to sleep, but the dream kept replaying itself and so she slipped on a robe and went downstairs to her study to write it down.

As she sat at her desk writing, she had the eerie feeling of being watched and turned quickly to see if John had followed her down. The draperies were drawn closed against the windows and everything was quiet except for the ticking of the mantle clock in the library and the electrical hum of her lamp. She looked with surprise at the last thing she had written: *It will not be necessary for me to visit you or for you to be aware of my presence in a phenomenal way. Rather assume that what you write has been guided by my unseen hand.*

She put her pen down and went back to bed.

     *   *   *

The change, at first, was imperceptible to Carol. Her original, draft outline depicted Franklin as a womanizer, lecher and sexist of the first order. Destroying him should be a piece of cake, Carol had thought. She wasn't even sure she wanted to spend the time doing this.

She reread her original outline, then tore it up in embarrassment. That approach wasn't quite right, she reasoned. Yet, when she attempted to come at her argument from a different angle, it likewise fell flat. Her research continued, but the writing came to a standstill. She didn't know what to say, until after the dreams began.

She got used to the subtle appearances of Franklin in her study as she worked. Nothing dramatic, just a sense of his presence and sometimes a vague image, (much like the time Wordsworth had visited her, she remembered): a hazy, adumbrated figure, recognizable but etheric. Conversation was telepathic and she got used to that too. She'd have a question as a thought, then as a thought, his answer came.

After a while, the extraordinary nature of these experiences became ordinary and she ceased to feel it was anything supernatural. Certainly she felt no fear. Rather, she began to look forward to the conversations with him, made comfortable with his presence by the dreams.

The change was in her feelings. Somewhere in the course of this project, the contempt she had for the man, the presumed sexist, dissipated, as she found no just cause in her readings. There were many anti-Franklin sentiments in the literature, but her observation skills were sharpened as she looked for the defense.

Chapter 6

Evans Library loomed as the focal point of the Bodley University campus, and Carol felt a warm familiarity every time she entered it. It had seven floors and over a million volumes. Architecturally it was square and unimaginative, but Carol felt the important thing about a library was what was inside, not the exterior, so her sense of pragmatism agreed with this austere design. She remembered a philosophy professor from her freshman year of college saying that as long as a college has a good library, you can get a decent education anywhere; you don't have to go to Harvard. Carol agreed, having all her life subscribed to the self-education method that a library offers.

She had a deep and abiding love for libraries and their quiet, hushed atmosphere. A library holds the secrets of all world knowledge, she mused; available to anyone, merely by opening a book. Carol couldn't remember a time when she didn't feel this sacred respect for libraries.

In second grade she voraciously read all the books available in her class-room. She couldn't believe the joy it brought her. When she had read near-ly all the books on the shelf, she experienced a kind of panic. What would she do when she read them all? Where would she get more? Did more books even exist? An observant teacher sensed her dilemma and suggested she join the town library. To seven-year old Carol, it was an unknown. What in fact was a library? The teacher gave her all the information she needed and on Saturday, Carol begged her mother to take her there. After that first visit, Carol was on her own. Her mother refused to spend every Saturday at the library, having other things to do. Carol had to plead with her mother for the independence of going alone. She boarded the bus that picked her up near her house and dropped her off downtown near the library. Taking the bus alone gave Carol a feeling of independence and maturity. She always sat in the very last seat by the window, curiously and unobtrusively observing everyone who got on and off. She made up names for them; she remembers naming one woman 'Sophie Tucker' for no apparent reason. She spoke to no one (having been taught like most children, to distrust strangers), and no one ever approached her. The solitary, serious child must have been a curiosity to other travelers.

When she first started her Saturday jaunts to the library, she was, because of her age, limited to the children's library on the second floor. You had to be twelve years old before you were allowed to use the adult section. Still, she found enough treasures in the children's library to satisfy her for the years until she was twelve. She'd climb the stairs to the second floor and pause a moment at the top of the steps, feeling a kind of overwhelm at the huge selection of books. She didn't know there was a system to find a particular book; she wandered from shelf to shelf feasting her eyes on the titles, occasionally pulling one from its place. As a child she read with no method or organization, with no advice from any adult. She picked books that interested her, reading on all subjects that caught her eye. When she found one section that yielded a good book, she systematically read everything on the same shelf, or the same subject or by the same author. Such was the random design of her designless reading.

She obeyed all the library rules: was silent, handled the books with great care, returned them on time and if they were late, she dutifully paid the pennies that were charged. She never wrote in books; covered them in the rain and in short treated them like precious treasures. When finding a ripped page, she carefully repaired it with tape, and if someone inconsiderately wrote in the books, she gently erased pencil marks. She took a sense of personal responsibility toward all library books.

She remembered the day she was twelve and was allowed to join the real library for the first time. She entered the room on the main floor with a ponderous sense of mission, ignored the steps leading to the children's library, to where she would never again return, and boldly walked in to the main library, half fearing she would be challenged, yet knowing she was entitled. After all, she was twelve. Skinny and short, her wavy blond hair halfway down her back, she looked no more than eight or nine, but she was twelve.

The adult library was daunting. The stacks were higher and it wasn't labeled as simply as the children's: "Biography, Fiction, Mystery." She slowly taught herself the Dewey decimal system by noting how the numbers increased even after the decimal point, how certain topics seemed to be grouped by number. With each new accumulation of knowledge about how libraries worked, she felt empowered, satisfied, eager for more.

By wandering these stacks she continued her random, wildly diverse education. In this way she discovered Wordsworth and fell in love with his Intimations of Immortality Ode. She found a book on the Profumo scandal and not knowing what it was, read it. That lead her to explore other books about English parliament and government. Her reading was a free association education. If she had had someone to guide her, there would have been more structure to her reading; but as it was, she was left alone to explore and develop this random education.

Later when she was in college and had to learn to use the card system, she discovered a whole new way of using libraries. This was glorious. Now, if she wanted to know everything about a certain subject, it was all grouped together for her, neatly, one card after another. The brief description was either an invitation to read further or to dismiss.

Still later, when libraries became computerized, she learned again to access all this knowledge in a faster and more efficient way. No matter what they did to the access system, libraries were still, to her, this vast and sacred storehouse of all knowledge accumulated by the human race, and she revered it. As long as the books were there, solid and bound in heavy covers, pages of type, millions of words, she was happy.

It was much later in her life that she discovered it was Benjamin Franklin who formed the first public lending library.

Today she quickly got the books she was looking for and unlocked her carrel in the library. She put her books and papers on the small shelf over the built-in desktop and sat in the chair. The tiny room was barely enough to turn around in, designed, of course for no distractions. Just you and the book.

Carol scanned the books for information about Franklin's early years, looking to see if there were clues in his childhood to the man he would become.

Chapter 7

When Josiah Franklin's brother, Benjamin arrived from England, it was a memorable event for young Benjamin, his namesake. Though the brothers had always been each other's favorite, they came to a falling out over young Ben.

Uncle Benjamin had literary leanings; he wrote verse and taught Ben to do so. Young Ben found he enjoyed verse-making immensely and spent hours with his uncle in literary endeavors. To practical Josiah, this was a sinful waste of time and he forbid young Ben to write such drivel. He also criticized his brother for being a bad influence on his son. (And why, while we're at it, don't you get a job?)

Ben was nine years old when his uncle arrived, and he responded to his uncle's story telling as an eager listener and a compatriot soul. A creative spark awakened within him and he dreamed of a future as a poet, a writer, a man of belle lettres.

"I wanted that badly," Ben said to Carol as he read over her shoulder.

She lifted her hands from the keyboard. "Why did you let your father dissuade you? You probably could have been a very successful poet."

He smiled at her gently. "Oh, I was. But not in that lifetime. You see, it wasn't my father who actually dissuaded me, though indeed he tried. He told me my poetry was awful, but, not being a man who had much tolerance for fancy words, I don't think he understood it. Therefore, his opinion on my verse was not the devastating comment it appears to be. No, it wasn't my father." He stared off dreamily, as if seeing something else.

Carol waited patiently, knowing he would speak only when he had something to say, and prompting from her usually just brought the gentle, and sometimes mysterious smile.

"I will tell you," he said finally, and she had the image of him pulling up a chair and making himself comfortable.

"I had enough of the rebel in me to defy my father had it been my true bent. Nay, defiance is the wrong word. I might have succeeded as a poet despite my father, and in truth I thought about it.

"One day, after my uncle and I had spent pleasant hours spinning tales and talking of poetry and such, I was alone in the wood behind my house. There was a tree with a large boulder upon which I sat, fancying myself in a rather melancholy mood, as I surmised was befitting a young poet."

Carol noted there was always that self-deprecating manner of speaking, as though he were amused by his human foibles.

"While contemplating on my chosen craft and imagining no doubt the brilliant verse I would compose upon a field of daisies, there suddenly appeared before me a strange and foreign man, dressed in a manner quite absurd for that time in Boston. I saw not from which direction he came for there wasn't a true path to my spot by the boulder, just a grassy field and yonder the house. I noticed him not one second before I saw him standing before me.

"His eyes were dark, yet gentle and knowing. He looked at me, I thought, with great compassion and said, 'Hello, Benjamin.'

"I thought it odd that a stranger to these parts would be so readily acquainted with my name and to speak in a tone at once intimate and fatherly. And yet, I felt no fear or ill- disposition toward the man. In fact, I was quite comfortable in his presence.

"'You must obey your father and give up poetry,' he said, and now I thought this queerer than ever, for I had discussed this inner conflict with no one. Did I mention his clothing? It was strange. He wore a maroon robe and sandals and carried a wooden staff. My thought was that he must be a wandering beggar of sorts, yet he carried no pack, and his demeanor was clean and alert, unlike a beggar.

"Most politely I questioned what concern my future was to him.

"'Your future most definitely concerns me, my son.' Those were his very words and as he said 'my son' with what appeared to be great love and compassion, I felt my heart contract inside me as though it would weep with some kind of perplexed joy and yearning.

"Then he told me this: 'In this lifetime, your destiny is clearly defined. Your mission is already determined, though you may not remember that determination of which you were a part. You will do many things, travel far and play an important role in the establishment of this country and its government. I am here to tell you that answering the poetic call within you will interfere with your chosen destiny. You must let it go willingly and follow the path that you agreed to before you came here.' So he spake.

"Well, my dear Carol, remember I was but a boy and the poetic muse was strong within me. Talk of a future and government meant little to me. I persisted and restated my love of poetry and my desire to pursue that avenue.

"With not another word, the man waved his hand at the space between my boulder and a coppice and the most wondrous sight appeared before my very eyes. It was a vision of what America would become." He held up his hand to Carol. "It would do no good to question me on that. I simply could not render it into words. I can tell you only that the vision was sufficient to convince me, where all his words could not, of the absolute and final certainty of my destiny and my part in this divine and glorious plan.

"The vision was meant to sustain me as I lived my life's mission. And sustain me it did."

Carol heard a dreamy quality in his voice as though he listened to a memory. She waited and then typed everything he just said into her computer. When she finished she wondered how he repressed the desire to be a poet.

"The good Master told me that it would come to pass. In a future life I could become the most excellent poet I craved to be, but truly I must let it go in this life. My destiny was written."

"Then, you had to obey his orders?" she asked hesitantly.

"It wasn't so much a dictum to be obeyed but a reminder of something to which I had already agreed."

After that he was silent for so long Carol thought he'd gone. She wanted to record those words before they slipped away, though her memory was cementing them rapidly.

"Did it come to pass?" she asked finally, hoping she was not talking to herself. "Did you become a famous poet?"

Then there was the gentle smile, looking at her as well as at the memory. "Indeed."

"Who was the man in the robe?"

"One of the great ones...spiritual masters who come to earth to help us, teach us, guide us, and guide the destiny of the universe." He shrugged, palms turned outward. "It would matter not for you to know his name. I saw him consciously three more times in that life, but always I felt his reassuring presence, though I could not see him. He told me things that convinced me he was one to obey as well as to trust. Let's leave it at that, my child."

"May I ask about your other life as a poet?"

"That lifetime is not pertinent to your book. Perhaps on another occasion we can discuss that." His smile was infectious and Carol felt her face responding in kind.

"Another book? On your life as a poet, Dr. Franklin?" She was teasing him.

He laughed heartily. "We'll see. But now, to the work at hand."

She turned back to the computer and reread what she'd written. If all this is true, she thought later as she turned off the computer, Benjamin

Franklin was a living monument to the ability of one man, when divinely inspired (as indeed he appears to have been) to be a vehicle for the spiritual force for the benefit of mankind. His contributions to humanity are so vast, she thought, he could not have been an agent for anything other than the divine force.

Chapter 8

Practically one of the first people Benjamin met when he arrived in Philadelphia at age sixteen was Deborah Read and her parents. He rented a room from them and became friends with Deborah who was two years younger than he.

In the summer of 1724, there was "sort of" a courting going on. He was eighteen, she sixteen. Later in life, he recalled they had great "affection" for one another at that time. Deborah's father died and Mrs. Read, wanting to do the right thing as a single parent, discouraged them from marrying, saying they were too young. Also, young Ben was about to set off on a journey to England, to obtain financing for a printing press, and perhaps they should wait until he returned. They agreed to postpone marrying, though they promised to write, and in 1724 he set sail for England.

One of the many personality traits Franklin was known for was his detachment, his tendency for 'out of sight, out of mind.' At various times throughout his life, his many friends complained that he forgot them as soon as he left them. (It seems to me, to be successful at living in the moment, to take life as it comes, to go with the flow, one has to have this quality of detachment.) He never got too attached to people, places, things. While some may criticize this quality, I see it as a virtue. He once said "Absence makes the heart grow...well, absent," which more or less summarizes his view on the subject.

During the two years he was gone, he wrote only one letter to Deborah, telling her he was not likely to return soon. A clear kiss-off, one might say. But given the understanding of this personality trait, it is perfectly natural for him to adapt to his present surroundings and let go of the past.

This two-year period that he spent in England was a time of growing, experimenting and experiencing life. Who of us can remember our own years of eighteen to twenty as being much different? He experienced sex for the first time, became bold with women, and, feeling his burgeoning sexuality, sowed many oats. (note to self: find another phrase, too colloquial).

In fairness, those times could be described as a time of dissipation (for those times.) Today, his activities would likely not raise an eyebrow. Later he referred to his "wild" behavior then as "erratum" of which he admitted he made many.

He failed to obtain the loans necessary for the equipment, having been deceived in his expectations by the governor of Pennsylvania who sent him on this fool's errand, and in 1726 he gave up and sailed home with a promise of a job clerking in a general store.

But, back to his debauchery for a moment. He paid for these errata, both in guilt and regret (and perhaps a case of clap). Ben was not, after all, an insensitive and callous youth. The man he was to become could not have behaved the way he did without self-recrimination and regret. At some point in his youth, he fathered an illegitimate son, William, who became Franklin's responsibility (as well as his pride and joy) and whom he never denied or shrugged off. (No dead beat dad here).

He was penitent about his two-year lapse of morals, not only because it was against his basic integrity, but also for what he did to Deborah. He knew he had behaved dishonorably. He had courted her, was somewhat committed to her, then betrayed his promise to her.

He set about making reparations.

In his absence, and after his letter to her which she took (rightly so) as dismissal, Deborah married someone else, who turned out to be a bigamist and a cad. He left Deborah and was never heard from again. She was greatly unhappy at the circumstances in her life and Franklin felt responsible for her unhappiness. Always a man of great ethical and moral integrity, he sorely felt he was to blame for this situation, though it was more self-blame than any-thing the Reads said or did. Mrs. Read felt it was her fault that she had for-bidden the youngsters to marry when they wanted to.

*His lust got him into this trouble, he recognized, and he resolved **never to fall into that trap again**. The absolute success of this commitment to himself can be judged later.*

First, he made a resolution to formulate a plan to regulate his future con-duct, and which he would live by the rest of his life. In short, he resolved to be "moral." This was at age twenty. How many of us would have the maturity to recognize our errata at that age and proceed to "shape up?"

The resolve was: to be frugal, rational, pay all debts, speak truth always, "give nobody expectations that are not likely to be answered," be sincere in words and actions, be amiable, speak ill of no man, not even in truth, but to excuse faults and speak good of everyone. (Van Doren.) This resolve was, for him, to be not only a man of his word, but one whose word was "Truth, Kindness and beyond reproach." A sizable commitment, yet he always strove (mostly successfully) to live up to it.

Back in Philadelphia, he worked in a general store, learning to keep accounts and sell goods. When the store owner died, Ben returned to his for-mer trade, printing, and worked (again) for Sam Keimer.

His commitment to right his wrongs was not all talk. The first thing he did in this regard was marry Deborah, despite the precarious legal status of her marriage. Since she could not obtain a divorce from a man who had disap-peared, she and Ben married in a common-law ceremony, which would pre-clude legal difficulties should the missing husband return. (He never did.)

*It's hard to deny that his intentions here are based on guilt rather than on a grand passion. He was determined to make repairs and he believed marry-ing her was the "right" thing to do. Nevertheless and regardless of what the rea-sons, it appears to have been a happy marriage, fulfilling in most ways to both of them. In his **Autobiography** he says they "throve together." Their letters to each other are affectionate, comfortable, intimate; clearly they delighted in each other.*

His absolute sincerity in wanting to correct his errata evolved into his master plan for self-improvement, which has been criticized on several levels. The virtues he wanted to attain were set down in a list and he was going to work on them one at a time until he mastered them. The list:

1. *Temperance—Eat not to fulness, drink not to elevation.*

2. *Silence—Speak not but what may benefit others or yourself, avoid trifling conversation.*

3. *Order—Let all your things have their places; let each part of your business have its time.*

4. *Resolution—Resolve to perform what you ought; perform without fail what you resolve.*

5. *Frugality— Make no expense but to do good to others or yourself—i.e. waste nothing.*

6. *Industry—Lose no time, be always employed in something useful, cut off all unnecessary action.*

7. *Sincerity—Use no hurtful deceit, think innocently and justly, and, if you speak, speak accordingly.*

8. *Justice— Wrong none by doing injuries, or omitting the benefits that are your duty.*

9. *Moderation—Avoid extremes, forbear resenting injuries as much as you think they deserve.*

10. *Cleanliness—Tolerate no uncleanliness in body, clothes, or habitation.*

11. *Tranquillity—Be not disturbed at trifles, or at accidents common or unavoidable.*

12. *Chastity—Rarely use venery but for health and offspring, never to dulness, weakness, or the injury of your own or anothers peace or reputation.*

13. *Humility—Imitate Jesus and Socrates.*

This last was added after he showed the list to a friend who suggested his pride could be tempered by humility. The willingness to add this, and to admit he might need to work on that too, is a kind of humility (methinks.)

Carl Van Doren talks about Franklin having three lives, perhaps four at this time in his life (ages twenty to twenty-six): First, his public life, which was only just being seeded. He was meeting important people and making contacts which would later bear fruit. He made an extremely favorable impression wherever he went and his public life continued to grow as long as he lived.

Second, was his inner life. He always reflected on his behavior, establishing guidelines for improving his morals. His goal to reach moral perfection was a lifelong quest and he lived by the guidelines he set for himself in this quest. His self-reflection then expanded to include the whole moral and physical world, on which he (and Poor Richard) commented.

Third was his working life; running his general store and printing press. And fourth, more nebulous, he was sage-in-training.

*Accusations of his "womanizing" continued until quite late in his life, but in fact, there is **absolutely no evidence in any history book to indict him on this count.** No evidence he was ever unfaithful to Debbie, no evidence of any sexual indulgence other than this pre-marriage period in England. Since there is quite a lot of evidence about all other aspects of his life, it is suspect to speculate with any conviction on this. He admitted to this period of errata and then swore never to fall into that again. Why would we doubt a man of his word? A man with his integrity? If he were sincere about attaining the other virtues (and he was), why would he be a hypocrite about Chastity?*

*Towards the end of his life he evaluated his list of virtues and felt he had mastered all of them except Frugality. **All of them except Frugality.***

In a letter to Juliana Ritchie, he said he observes One Rule: "to be concern'd in no Affairs that I should blush to have made publick." (Wright p. 288.)

*Would Ben Franklin lie? He's not, let's remember, George Washington. Trust me, he's **not** George Washington.*

Chapter 9

Shortly after Debbie and Benjamin married they set up housekeeping on Market Street, opening a general store and a printing press next door.

William's birth date is unknown, but he is about two years old at this time. Though there is some evidence that Debbie didn't like him later in his life, there is none that she did not live up to her promise to Ben to raise him as her own son.

She and Ben worked side by side in the store, dealing with customers, keeping accounts, working hard, "thriving together." Debbie was friendly but with a sharp tongue, (so history says.) In today's world she'd probably be called aggressive and independent. She loved her husband and their personal relationship must have been satisfying to both of them. Franklin's writings from this period reflect a contented, satisfied man.

The store was successful under Debbie's careful management, as was the printing business Ben ran. Life was good. There were no financial hardships and friends were plentiful. Two years after they married, their son Francis Folger was born and both parents doted on him; Debbie with her brusque affection, Ben with his gentle sternness. One can only imagine their pain when this beloved child died at age four of smallpox. Franklin had been an outspoken proponent of inoculation, a new and experimental procedure for combating smallpox. His remorse that he hadn't been able to get little Franky inoculated, was lifelong.

Still, both Deborah and Ben were practical people and life goes on, even after the death of a child. They turned their energies to their store and work, soothing each other when alone, over this loss. Another criticism of Franklin is that "he took death well." How this is a flaw is beyond me, but I suppose if he had fallen apart at his son's death, this would have been a virtue? He was, remember, a natural stoic who accepted life as it came, wisely knowing it was impossible to fight the currents of fate. He didn't get angry at God for taking his child, nor did he rail against the fates, nor respond to this blow by wailing, "Why me?" Acceptance and detachment were stylistic devices that sprang from a natural well within him.

It would be another seven years before Debbie was pregnant again, giving birth in 1743 to their daughter, Sarah. Sally delighted both of them and helped fill the void left by their son's death.

Benjamin's interests outside his marriage were primarily intellectual: his beloved Junta, a club he formed with other men which met to discuss issues, inventions, social reform, ideas, experiments. His scientific experiments were done in his home, to Deborah's great tolerance. She was, for the most part, a typical 18th century woman: uneducated, practical, accepting the husband as "master of the house," though her strong personality would certainly preclude that she was in any way subservient to him. Though they were not intellectual equals, she appears to carry her own in other ways…being his companion, his helpmate, his bedmate…compatible undoubtedly in all these areas.

There is no record of discord or difficulty between them. When they were apart (fifteen of the last eighteen years of their marriage,) letters are affectionate. When together, there was harmony. He had, it seems, a great deal of wisdom in handling women in general, so it's not surprising he knew how to keep his wife happy. Poor Richard said, "Keep your eyes wide open before marriage, half closed after."

If, as reports say, Debbie was a shrew, Ben closed his eyes and his ears wisely, keeping peace and ignoring what could not be changed. He disliked contentions. He was a peaceable man who probably found it wise to give into her.

Thus, though others found her shrill, to him she was loving and devoted. She respected and admired her husband as much as the rest of the country did.

As frugal as her husband, Debbie however, never resented the expenditures Ben made on his experiments or the money he gave to various relatives and friends who sought his help. On one occasion she bought a silver bowl for him saying her husband deserved to eat out of such a fine bowl.

Debbie had absolute trust and confidence in her husband. In the first five years they were apart (1757-62), he lived in England in the home of Margaret Stevenson, a widow, and her daughter, Polly. Debbie never questioned his loyalty and faithfulness to her, nor doubted his goodness. Though there were speculations that his relationship with his landlady was of a "personal" nature, Debbie didn't believe it and nothing in their letters even gives voice to these rumors. Nor is there a shred of evidence to indicate otherwise.

Franklin may have been an outrageous flirt most of his life, but he was not an adulterer. He betrayed Debbie once before their marriage and he vowed never to do it again. If we know nothing else about Benjamin Franklin, we know he was an honorable man of his word. Throughout his life he stuck judiciously to his strict moral and ethical code in all areas of his life, including this one.

If he were guilty of some of these accusations, how could there never have been any rumor of sexual exploits? There's always rumor when someone fools around.

Carol paused, doubting the truth of the words she wrote. She remembered her own infidelity to John and knew it was possible to be so discreet that there were no rumors. Except, of course, the betrayed party knew. She felt a pang of regret remembering that period of her marriage, then quickly put the thought away. It was in the past.

Still, maybe Ben and Mrs. Stevenson were so discreet that there never was a breath of rumor. Debbie, after all, was thousands of miles away, across the ocean. No telephones, no instant communication. No department cocktail parties, she thought ruefully. Another world. Maybe it was possible. I should just ask him, she thought, going back to her notes.

The only behavior history has proof of is his flirtatiousness. This was not a secret. His wife knew of his many female friends and correspondents, yet she was not concerned. He was affectionate with all people, fatherly to younger women and gallant to all other women. Women responded in kind, showering him with platonic yet flirtatious, affection.

The only problem in this argument, Carol thought, pushing back from her desk and leaning her head back in her arms, is Mrs. Stevenson. They lived together, after all, for a total of sixteen years. It almost begs belief to say there was no hanky panky in all that time. No. 'Hanky panky' wouldn't define the kind of relationship he would have. He would consider Mrs. Stevenson his "wife." (Maybe that justified a sexual relationship?)

She contemplated the facts: he went to England in 1757, lived there five years, came home for two years (1762-64), then returned for eleven more years. I could argue either way: yes, he most definitely had a sexual relationship with Mrs. Stevenson. Would he have gone eleven years without sex? Puhleeze! If he considered her his "wife" he would not view their relationship as illicit or immoral. She would have been an expedient solution. Debbie, after all, was out of sight, Mrs. Stevenson was present. Discretion would be absolute, (for Debbie's sake). He would never divorce Debbie, his loyalty to her was too deep. Yet, they had been married thirty-four years by 1764; a long time in any era. It's logical to say he outgrew her; she didn't, after all, grow intellectually as he did. She was not his equal intellectually or socially. Could a spirit as spacious as Franklin be confined to one woman, one relationship for a lifetime? After such a long marriage (forty-four years by the time she died) what was left to say between them? Toward the end their letters became perfunctory and eventually Debbie stopped writing. Franklin had a lifelong habit of distancing himself from people who became an encumbrance, according to Lopez. No confrontations; just slip away. Is this what happened to his marriage?

"Duty" took him to England, indeed, but what a cover, what an excuse to set up another "marriage;" to never have to leave the first one or confront the issues. Simply leave it, maintain an affectionate correspondence, promise always to return home (but never do until she's dead.)

Debbie was not a passion, but then, neither was Margaret Stevenson. Debbie was reparation; Margaret was convenient, available, (discreet?) To consider Margaret his "wife" would be the only morally logical explanation according to Franklin's ethics. Debbie was a fond memory, an occasional yearning, but no longer a presence in his life. Franklin lived in the moment.

Debbie never deserved his betrayal or rejection, therefore he gave neither. Ben went on being kind to her (from afar), but he did indeed move on in life. Mrs. Stevenson corresponded with Debbie, reported on the good doctor, and they exchanged gifts. After Debbie died, did Margaret expect Franklin would marry her? And was she disappointed he did not? Is this just hindsight speculation? Historical speculation? Even now, as I speculate (or will you tell me, Ben?) the secret you hold about your sexual behavior during the years apart from your wife?

Her chair creaked as she leaned farther back, putting her feet up on her desk.

Argument two: Celibacy is entirely possible, despite his reputation as a ladies man. Franklin was a man who lived behind his image (the illusion of his image) all his life. He appeared to be a ladies man but was he all talk? There are at least two recorded instances of women who took his flirtatious proposition at his word and attempted to take it one step further (one step closer to the bedroom). He backed off quickly in both cases; the first time citing Debbie as his dearly beloved, the second (when he was a widower) with an excuse that the nights were not long enough. One can see the joy of flirtation is not necessarily enhanced by the further complication of consummating the flirtation. So, yes, it was entirely possible that Franklin was always faithful to his wife and that once she died he gave up sex entirely. Is it probable? I don't know. Masturbation is not a twentieth century invention; perhaps he was self-sufficient in that manner also.

During her last few years, Debbie was desperate for her husband to come home. She wanted to see him once more before she died. She'd had a stroke and was growing weak and enfeebled. It sounds heartless that he ignored her illness and kept promising to return soon. In fact, his business was more or less concluded two years earlier. Why *did* he stay in England those last two years?

Debbie was too far in the past; she was remote to both his present life and to his heart. She was a memory. Her death was no more than a blip in his life at that point. Perhaps in his mind she was already gone from him; the death was just a formality. The year 1774 had been (probably) the most difficult year of his life with his public humiliation and political failure, and ousting from England. Debbie was 66 years old and he had not seen her in ten years.

He wasn't at all heartless or cruel; merely detached. He gave her his best but he had long since moved on from her. She was out of his sight; it was only natural (to him) that she fell out of his mind.

Chapter 10

Carol and John met at a party when they were graduate students at Northwestern. She had just started in the Ph.D. program in Linguistics; John was in English. It was 1970 and the typical college party offered wine, beer, marijuana and LSD. Like most of her peers, Carol enjoyed getting high occasionally, but she always drew the line at experimental drugs, which she considered anything other than marijuana. That night she was late getting to the party, having spent most of the evening in the library. Leaving the library, she ran into Jim Baird, a fellow student, and invited him to go with her. He had a car, so she drove with him.

By the time they got there, the party was in full swing. Janis Joplin was on the stereo, belting out "Piece of my Heart," candles provided most of the lighting and people stood around in groups talking, smoking joints and drinking. Carol accepted a beer and a hit on someone's joint. She exchanged greetings with several people she knew and looked around the dimly lit room. She took another hit and wandered through the house, feeling the beginnings of mellow. In the kitchen, Toni, one of the people who lived in this house was carefully arranging a plate of sugar cubes. Several others stood around talking, watching Toni with varying degrees of interest.

"Here, Carol, you can be the first; we're going on a trip." She was already high and sounded kind of spacey as she held the plate of LSD-laced sugar cubes in front of Carol. Carol smiled and looked at the plate as though deciding which one to take. Then she wrinkled her nose at Toni.

"Maybe later." She held up her beer to indicate this was enough at the moment. Toni shrugged and carried the tray into the other room. Carol noticed a man standing nearby, light brown hair, curly and long, smiling at her. He seemed amused at her pretense of taking acid. She shrugged her shoulders at him turned and walked out of the kitchen. Leaning against the doorway was a red-haired man with a broad forehead looking at her through half-closed eyes. "Oh, baby, this is great, come with me." He reached out and grabbed her arm.

She shook her head, smiling and pushed off his hand. "In your dreams." She went into the living room again. Several people had taken the sugar cubes and were starting to trip. One guy sank soundlessly to the floor, a beatific smile on his face. She stepped over him as she saw an empty spot on the couch, next to some people she knew. They were passing a joint and she accepted it when it reached her.

"Hey, Carol, how's it going?"

"OK, Dave, how's it with you? PJ here?"

"No, she's pissed at me for something. Punishing me by not coming." He laughed and held his side, "Oooh I'm suffering."

The others laughed and Carol realized she was far too sober to enjoy this party. Then another linguistics student arrived late and sat on the arm of the couch and started talking to her. Like her, he wasn't stoned, so she passed an hour of good conversation with him, had another beer, then decided it was time to go home.

She stood up to leave, tossing her hair over her shoulder. At twenty-four, Carol's style was typical of the times. Her long blond hair hung straight, or as straight as naturally wavy hair could, and she wore the uniform bell-bottom jeans and shaggy sweater. Like most of her female friends, she wore no makeup, the natural look being vogue. Though she was pretty, her figure and her looks were fairly average. It was the sparkle in her eyes that one noticed. Her hazel eyes that sometimes looked greener shone with clear intelligence and humor.

She looked around for Jim to see if he wanted to leave, since he was her ride. Tired and bored she was ready to go home and get some sleep. As she scanned the room her eyes met a pair of gentle, smiling and she unconsciously noted, sober, eyes. She gave a half-smile as she realized it was the guy from the kitchen with the long, curly hair. She glanced away as he approached.

"Are you looking for me?" he asked.

"I don't know. Are you the guy I came with?"

He pretended to think about it. "I don't think so, but I think I'm the one you should leave with."

She laughed. "Nice try. Oh, there he is." She saw Jim who had apparently lost no time catching up with the party. He was flying. The front of his shirt was wet from spilled beer and he was talking loud. He looked disgusting.

"Is he someone special?" the man asked with a straight face looking at Jim and back to Carol.

Carol squinted her eyes at Jim and held her chin as though deciding. "I don't know, what do you think?" They both laughed.

"So, what's a nice girl like you doing at a party like this?"

She laughed again, "What makes you think I'm nice?"

"I can smell a nice girl a mile away."

"Oh, and what does a nice girl smell like?"

He leaned closer and sniffed. "Lilacs? Roses? Budweiser?" She liked his humor and she thought he was cute. His hair wasn't quite to his shoulders but the cascading curls were gorgeous. He was tall, with a lanky build and nice brown eyes, soft and warm. She looked at that first when she met someone. She got a feel for people from their eyes.

"I'm John Byrd."

"Carol Throgmorton."

"And you are definitely *not* attached to him?" He gestured with his beer bottle toward Jim.

"Most definitely not."

"So…what sign are you?"

"Uh uh. That's a bad line. Maybe I should just walk home."

"I'm sorry. I'm trying to impress you and I'm not sure how."

"Astrology isn't the way."

"OK. Um, how about this? I'm finishing my doctorate in Medieval literature."

She nodded, "Much better. That worked."

He wiped his forehead in mock relief. "Whew. What about you?"

"Linguistics. But my undergrad is Lit."

"Linguistics, huh? That makes you more scientist than poet."

She smiled.

"Am I forgiven for my bad lines? I've wanted to meet you ever since I saw you in the kitchen." He seemed kind of shy and unsure of himself and Carol found that appealing. "Do you want to get out of here? Maybe go somewhere for coffee?"

She thought about it for two seconds, then said yes.

They went to an all-night diner and ordered coffee. Two hours later they ordered sandwiches and three hours after that they ordered breakfast. They talked continuously, each delighted to discover someone they liked. By the time he drove her home it was almost five a.m.

In the weeks that followed they began spending a lot of their free time together. As students they had very little money, but there were so many free things to do on campus, it didn't matter. John didn't seem in any hurry to get involved romantically or sexually and this perplexed Carol. She wandered if he was ever going to kiss her and began to fear he wanted to be just friends. Maybe he had a girlfriend back home. They were studying at his apartment one night and she decided to ask him.

"No," he said looking at her curiously. "Why do you ask?"

She felt her skin get hot. "I just wondered, you know...why you haven't..."

"Kissed you?" he asked softly.

"Yes."

He sat next to her on the couch and put one arm around her. He ran his finger lightly on her face and her skin tingled. He brought his face close to hers and looked into her eyes.

"I think you're someone special and I was just waiting for the right time," he said softly. "Timing is everything, you know." She parted her lips slightly and waited.

His mouth was close, "Do you want me to kiss you now?" His tone was teasing.

"I don't really care," she said reaching her arms up, "I just want to get my hands in that hair."

The kissing was so good they decided to continue it in the bedroom.

Chapter 11

Three months into their relationship, John told her he was in love with her. Carol was a little scared by this declaration, not knowing for sure if she felt the same. She valued their friendship and their intellectual compatibility and was happy they agreed on most social and political issues. Sexually she enjoyed him tremendously. But love? She just didn't know if that fit into her academic future at the present.

Carol stoically assumed they would go their separate ways when they left Northwestern. John was nearly finished writing his dissertation and was job-hunting. When he landed a position at Bodley, Carol was relieved that at least for the next year, they'd be able to see each other on weekends. Numen wasn't that far from Northwestern. Her fear was that her own job hunt would take her to another part of the country and that would make the relationship impossible.

Not every college had a linguistics department and some didn't even offer courses in it. Carol knew her job search would be limited to certain colleges.

During the next year, John began teaching at Bodley and Carol often visited him on weekends, or he drove to Northwestern to be with her. She dreaded the thought of them eventually parting, but being practical, she knew that unless by some miracle Bodley offered her a job (they did not have a linguistics department), she might have to be in a different part of the country. For the most part, they avoided discussing this possibility, living instead in the moment.

On one of the weekends she drove to Numen to be with John, he was preparing for a Chaucer course, teaching *Troilus and Cressida*. He wanted to reread it that weekend. Carol would have rather spent the time making love, but knew he had to prepare.

"I'll read it with you," she said stretching out next to him on the couch."

"Aw, c'mon, don't make this hard for me," he said opening the book.

"Ooh, but I love to make it hard for you," she said suggestively.

"Carol," he said helplessly, kissing her, "later. I really do have to read this."

"OK, OK. Let's read it out loud and we'll alternate pages. OK? Are you reading in middle English or translation?"

"Translation. It's an undergraduate course."

Soon they were both absorbed in the story. She liked better the melodious cadence of middle English, which they both read fluently, but even in modern English this retained some of the feel of Chaucer's rhythm.

After awhile she fell silent, a frown on her face. John nudged her, "Your turn."

"You read, I'm thinking."

He drew back to look at her quizzically, and saw the look of concentration on her face.

He continued reading and was nearly at the end when he paused and felt the peace of the moment; reading something he enjoyed with the woman he loved, soft and warm in his arms. He let the book rest on his chest and kissed the top of her head. He'd read enough for now, maybe he could rekindle Carol's earlier mood. He reached for the buttons on her shirt and kissed her hair again.

"That pimp! That's what he is. Some uncle." She sat up abruptly.

"Carol, what are you talking about?"

"Pandarus," she said as though they'd just been discussing him. "Don't you see? Here's his niece, Cressida whom he should be protecting. Instead, he's arranging to have her delivered to Troilus to be sexually ravished. He's a frigging pimp. I never saw it this way before."

"But she loves Troilus...or will when..."

"When what? When he rapes her?" She waved him away. "She doesn't love him...she's terrified, trapped. I never saw it this way before," she said almost to herself. "I want to get these thoughts on paper before I lose it." She went to the kitchen table with a notebook and pen and started writing, oblivious to John.

She wrote a critique on Pandarus as pimp, Troilus as a john and Cressida as the enforced whore. It was published in an experimental, feminist journal and caused somewhat of a stir in academic circles. Chaucer, like Shakespeare, was one of the sacred cows, held above negative criticism.

John was proud of her publication but disagreed with her thesis.

"Carol, you know if you're going to attack a king, you have to kill him."

"Oh, John, I'm not attacking Chaucer. I just took a different approach to interpreting *Troilus and Cressida*. I love Chaucer, I do."

"What do you call this, then, feminist criticism?"

She smiled, taking the journal from him, "Yeah. Do you like it?"

He shook his head smiling. "You're incredible. Yes, I like it. I like you. Come here."

She wrapped her arms around his waist and tilted her head back for his kiss.

He kissed her then looked at her. "Will you marry me?"

"What?"

"I said will you marry me?" His eyes were serious. "It can't be that much of a surprise, Carol. We've been together for almost two years. I'm in this for keeps, you know."

She pulled away from him. "John, you've got a job at Bodley and I don't. If I don't work at the university, there's nothing in Numen for me."

"There's me," he said, trying to be cute, realizing as soon as he said it that it was a mistake.

"I didn't go to school for twenty years to be just a wife and maybe work at Burger King," she said coldly.

"What's Burger King? A symbol for the oppressed woman?"

"It's a symbol for what kind of work I can do if I don't do what I've been trained for. You can't really expect me to give that up for marriage, do you?"

"Don't turn this into a feminist argument. This was a marriage proposal because I love you. Remember?" He was hurt and angry.

"I love you too, John. But I can't give up everything I've worked for to be with you. I just can't." She looked pained, but determined as she took a deep breath. "I was going to tell you this weekend, but you, you sprang this on me...I..I've been offered at job at Columbia."

He looked at her, stunned. "Columbia...as in New York?"

She nodded numbly and said nothing.

"I thought...I mean...we'd be together. I thought you wanted that too."

"I do, John, I really do, but I don't see how. Bodley has had my vitae for two months. It apparently doesn't have any need for me and I don't know what else I can do. I can't marry you and go to New York."

He drew a deep breath and looked at her steadily. "If Columbia is where you want to go, so be it. I'm sure there are plenty of Burger Kings in New York where I can work."

Her eyes filled with tears. "Oh, John, you'd do that for me? But I can't let you give up your job here."

"Oh, Carol. I can get another job. But I don't want another woman. I want you."

So they were married and it turned out Carol's Chaucer article made the difference at Bodley; Burger King was not to be in her future. Once the buzz about her *Troilus and Cressida* article got around, she was actually courted by several colleges, Bodley being one, who wanted to keep her in the State. John mentioned to the Chair that she was his fiancée, hoping to strengthen her claim, and so she was offered a job teaching the history of the English language and semantics while she developed a linguistics course. They also wanted her to develop and teach a feminist criticism course.

In her concluding interview in which the position was offered to her, she complimented the Chairman, "Dr. Waring, you are a very progressive man."

"Thank you, Dr. Throgmorton," he said wryly. "I'm also married to a very progressive woman." Carol surmised from this comment that his wife might have had some influence in this job offer. Carol didn't care. She was delirious that she got a job at Bodley, and that she and John would be together.

Though they never discussed it again, they both were aware of the uncomfortable possibility that John loved her more than she loved him. She knew (and was grateful) that John would have worked at Burger King if that were the only way they could be together. Carol, on the other hand, would never have considered moving to Numen without a job at the college. She would have gone off to Columbia, missed John briefly, and then got over him. Not one to cling to romantic notions, she would have pragmatically set about a new life without him.

Chapter 12

One thing John admired about Carol was her innate sense of freedom. She had no prohibitive, guilt-inducing inhibitions. She treated her body and its functions as very natural and normal. This included sex. He always found this quality enviable and secretly it awed him.

He remembered when they first met and how impressed he was with her sense of self. He would have been embarrassed at turning down the LSD at the party, so he avoided the person offering it. When he saw Carol politely but firmly refuse, causing no loss of face for herself or the one offering it, he was impressed.

When they began seeing each other, Carol was so open and direct that he found himself a little intimidated by her. How could he possibly make a romantic move on her when she gave no indication she wanted it? She was extremely intelligent with a sharp, no-nonsense attitude, and he thought maybe she preferred that they were just friends. If he made a move and she refused him, it would be like the drugs at the party...a polite but firm rejection, and he'd feel like a jerk. So he waited.

When she asked if he had a girlfriend and why didn't he kiss her, John was flooded with relief. Yes, she wanted it. He kissed her gratefully and warmly, then passionately as she kept receiving and returning his kisses.

He had never known a girl so openly frank about enjoying sex. She treated it, and by extension, him and what he offered, as a gift that brought her much pleasure.

Once when they had talked about it, she said she thought God surely must have given us sex for pleasure, to enjoy. Procreation aside, this was a gift from the heavens. What better way to show appreciation for a gift, she reasoned, than to enjoy it fully in gratitude and pleasure.

She had no guilt where God or sex was concerned.

John's restrictive Catholic upbringing left him with inhibitions about sex and his body. Nothing too debilitating; just enough guilt to make him a little self-conscious around women. He marveled that though Carol's background was similar, she wasn't burdened with the guilt and inhibitions as he was. After a few years with her, he had managed to shed a lot of his hang-ups and he was grateful to her for her part in this. She still had a down-to-earth attitude about sex; do it if it feels good. He marveled and delighted in her open enjoyment of making love with him and he was glad she was his wife.

In the first months of their sleeping together, they talked about their religious backgrounds and the repressive approach to sex.

"I thought the church had to be wrong about sex," she told him. "It was wrong about so many other things."

"But where did you get that idea...that the church could be wrong?"

She shrugged. "I figured it out myself. I mean, so much of what I was taught just didn't make sense, so I started relying on my own logic. This is kind of hard to explain," she said, making a face. "I never verbalized it before. Didn't you ever question the church's authority?"

"I guess not. I didn't believe a lot of the stuff, but I don't think I looked for an alternative. I guess I figured someone had to be the authority. I didn't challenge that."

"But you see, that's where I had a problem with the Church. Why should I allow anyone to have authority over me? If there's something I know to be true, why should I doubt myself in favor of someone else's reasoning? Does God love the priests more than me? I didn't believe that."

"The church speaks for God via the Pope we were taught."

"Yeah, well, I didn't buy that. I think it's just a power play to keep people down, keep us subservient to the priests. I believe God loves me as much as he loves the Pope, so why should he give truth to the Pope and not to me? I found my own connection for getting truth and it didn't depend on an intermediary."

"What you're saying makes sense, but it seems…well, arrogant to assume you're the same as the pope."

"Not the same, that's not what I'm saying…just not lesser in God's eyes. That's all I'm saying."

"So, tell me how you get answers if you don't believe what the church says." They had just made love and were lying in his bed on their backs. He stretched his arms behind his head and leaned back against the wall.

"Hmm…it's kind of hard to explain *knowing*. It's like a feeling that is confirmed. OK, suppose someone says to you, 'the earth is flat.' Do you blindly accept this statement as true because an Authority said it? What I do is, not necessarily reject it, but question it. I put it on my truth meter and take a reading."

"A truth meter?" he said laughing.

"Yeah. I see how that statement hits me…as truth, lie, or somewhere in between. Truth gives me a certain feeling of clarity, sort of like, oh, like a bell ringing. A lie is at the other end; it resonates inside me like a non-feeling or clunk. This is very subjective, I know, but I can't explain it any other way. Do you see?"

He looked at her intently, knowing there was something important to learn here, but he was having a hard time understanding, since he had no such reference point.

"So you would decide whether or not the earth was flat based on your own knowledge about the earth?"

"No, it's more of a feeling thing. No matter how much reasoning the argument has, inside is the *feeling* that No, it's wrong and the earth is not flat. And that's what I go with. I live my life by this inner…I don't know…it's like an unspoken guidance. Like there's someone or some force that is directing me to do what's right or what's best. It's very vague, but reliable for me."

"Do you mean like *God*?" He was trying to understand if this was a religious thing for her. She laughed and turned to him and tweaked his nose.

"I don't know about that. It's sort of practical and, well, just *there*. The first time I remember being conscious of this I was about twelve. My mother had just told me to do something...I think I accepted a friendship ring from a boy and she told me I was too young and had to give it back. This law she was laying down was so *anti* what I was feeling that I told her I would not listen to her and that I was keeping the ring. I was very firm about this, very sure what I was doing was right. Jeez, I was twelve. It's not like I got engaged or anything. It meant this boy liked me and I liked him. Period."

"What did she do?"

"Nothing. She never said a word back to me. Something happened in that moment. We looked at each other, I, in my defiance, ready for battle over this. She simply ceded. At the time, regarding it as a battle, I would have said she lost. I think she knew, given my stubborn and rebellious streak, that I wouldn't have listened, so she saved her breath. I don't know. Maybe there was something wise in her decision...I just never gave her credit for that." She stayed silent for a few minutes, thinking back to that time.

"After that I knew I, and not my parents, was in charge of making my decisions. It took me years to recognize the significance of that moment. I was going to be in control of my life, not any authority outside of me, not even my parents. As I got older, it always appalled me how many people *accepted* so readily someone else's authority over them: church, government, a boss, a uniform, a spouse. I mean, everybody has this inner connection, if only they knew. So, why are people so afraid to use it, to trust themselves?"

"And you're saying your parents simply let you make all your own decisions, all through your teenage years?" he asked, unbelieving.

"Pretty much." She nestled her head into his shoulder and pulled up the sheet, yawning, "I made good decisions; maybe that's why they didn't hassle me too much." He smiled in the dark kissing her hair.

"Loving me is a good decision."

"Best one I ever made," she said sleepily.

Often, over the years, he marveled at the way she was able to do that, get that inner guidance. Her impressions of people, decisions about anything, were rarely wrong and he had to agree, sometimes reluctantly, that this intuitive cognition she had, was nearly always right.

Early in their marriage there was a new professor in the history department with whom John became friendly. He and his wife and Carol and John got together socially and though John was impressed with them, Carol sensed something else. She told John she did not want to get too friendly with them.

"But, Carol, I like them."

"Well, I don't. There's something about them I don't trust."

"What did they do? What don't you like about them?"

"OK, if you want to know, I get the feeling they're sleazy."

He laughed. "That is absolutely ridiculous. You really think you're never wrong about people, but this time you are."

They argued over whether to see them again, and though Carol's suspicion of them did not abate, they did socialize with them again. Until the night Bert (the husband) cornered Carol in the kitchen and made a pass at her, assuring her that this is what John and Ella were doing in the living room.

Carol shoved him out of the way and pushed the door into the living room. Sure enough, Ella was on John's lap and it looked as though they were wrestling. John gave Carol a look of enormous relief as Carol, with icy control, told them to leave, that she and John were not interested in swapping.

As she slammed the door behind them she turned to John, her voice still icy. "I assume I was speaking for both of us?"

"Are you crazy? Of course. I had no idea they were into that kind of thing." She didn't say another word, nor did they ever discuss it again. John gave her the opportunity to say I told you so, but she didn't take it, and he was grateful.

After that, he was more respectful of her intuition.

Chapter 13

When Carol and John bought the house in Numen, they had starry-eyed ideas about restoring it to its original Victorian splendor. Stripping the oak wood down to its original skin was the easy part. Old plumbing and old electrical wiring began causing inconveniences neither of them had much tolerance for. The first winter they discovered the inadequate insulation. They installed a Franklin stove in the fireplace in the living room and did a lot of taping the drafty spots at windows and doors. The following spring they bought bales of pink, fiberglass insulation and crawled on their hands and knees in the attic, spreading it between the beams.

"We'll put six inches more than suggested," John said.

Next they hired an electrician to completely rewire the house. That cost set them back on improvements and they halted their renovations for lack of money. They started re-evaluating the value of restoration. Wouldn't modernization work just as well?

In the spring they began the outdoor work. On their property was an old garage and a shed, both filled with what they considered junk. They cleaned out both and threw away most of it. They repaired the garage so their cars could be kept there. John built shelves in the shed and they organized what tools they had. He was inordinately proud of his handiwork.

Carol discovered that underneath the overgrown grass and weeds was brick. She followed it and found it was a brick pathway winding around the back of the house and it led to a small, brick patio by a dirty pond, nearly hidden by the shrubbery overgrown around it. The water was low and stagnant and she had visions of cleaning it out and putting fish there. Carol began by pulling the weeds that had grown between and around the bricks, nearly obscuring them. Wearing gloves and kneeling on a pad, she worked for hours each weekend, all through the summer, pulling weeds and clearing the patio one brick at a time.

"I'm reclaiming the patio from the weeds," she said grandly to John.

"You know, honey, weed killer will do that job in a lot less time," John stood over her holding a rake.

"No, I don't want to use chemicals," she said firmly.

"It'll take you forever to get all the weeds."

She sat back and wiped the sweat from her forehead with the back of her hand.

"I'll never get all the weeds," she agreed. "That's not what this is about." She squinted up at him past the rim of the straw hat she wore.

"Pray tell, what *is* this about then?" He squatted down next to her.

"John," she said patiently. "Weeds are like the unconquerable worm. I know it's impossible to get them all. I pull one and ten more grow. But to pull each one up by the roots, knowing it was a fair struggle and I won, well, it gives me a feeling of accomplishment."

"So it's not the end result you care about, it's the journey," he teased.

"It's like, this may sound silly, but the weeds are a metaphor for the things in me that I'd like to pull out. You know, the ugly things," she wrinkled her nose at him.

"Sweetheart, you don't have ugly things in you."

She threw a handful of dirt at him. "See? I do too. I know I'll never win, but I have to keep trying." She said it solemnly but with a stubbornness he was familiar with.

John knew better than to argue with her, even about something like her flaws. During their first year of marriage when there are so many adjustments to be made, John learned that he was the one who had to do most of the adjusting if he wanted to keep things peaceful. Carol was a strong, independent woman who, as a member of the first graduating class of the women's movement, was not about to be controlled by a man and which she let him know in no uncertain terms. John argued that he didn't want to control her, and though she believed him because he was not that kind of man, she nevertheless felt she had to assert her independence by making her own decisions and when necessary, going against his wishes for the sake of assertion. John found it wiser to let himself be amused by her personality traits rather than offended. It was going to be key to the success of their marriage. She knew that he would not interfere with her personal freedom but that he might laugh at her. She accepted that. Humor was a preferable way of dealing with their differences. She tried to remember that when John did things that irritated her.

After three years of marriage, much of the adjustment was complete and their roles in place. In marriage, you either adapt and accept the other's personality or you start getting in trouble. John was learning that it was best to give her space and let her be, and though there were things he would like to be different, for the most part he accepted her for who and what she was. By nature he was not as aggressive or competitive as she, so it wasn't a difficult adjustment on his part. He was content to love her, be proud of her and enjoy his own accomplishments and satisfactions in his career.

Carol, for her part, mellowed a little with time. She knew she had in John, the perfect mate for her. He let her do her thing without judgment and criticism. He was supportive of her feminist activities and encouraged her to full expression of this. He truly wasn't threatened by her and she was both grateful and proud of him.

"You are very secure in your maleness," she told him one night in bed, fondling his maleness. "I like that in a man."

For as sharp-edged, cool and distant as Carol could be when they were at work or in public, alone in their home and in bed she was loving and passionate and did not leave John in any doubt that she desired and appreciated him. It helped him to overlook some of the other things about her that irritated him. He watched her one night when she was giving a lecture to a women's group, and he thought of how she had been in bed with him last night, eager and tender and in her moment of orgasm, totally his. He smiled to himself and felt a warm rush of gratitude and satisfaction that she was his wife.

*   *   *

Years later in the first months after her affair ended, when there was a painful strain between them, John found her in the garage one warm spring day, going through the shelves.

"What are you looking for?" he asked.

"The poison that kills the weeds," she said without turning around.

"Why? You're not weeding by hand this year?" He reached up to a higher shelf and pulled down a bottle.

"No, it'll take forever that way." He mixed the poison into a large spray bottle and said he would do it for her.

"Good," she said walking back to the house, "just kill all the fucking weeds."

Chapter 14

"Carol, wake up, it's six-thirty." Her mother shook her and Carol turned over groaning. Then she snapped to attention.

"Six-thirty?" she said out loud. If she didn't get up immediately, she'd be off schedule. She threw back the covers and ran down the hall to the bathroom, finding the door closed; her sister had beat her to it.

"How long will you be?" she called with some urgency in her voice.

The door opened and her sixteen-year old sister glared at her, "Twerp,"she said as she brushed past her.

Carol ignored her and went into the bathroom, quickly washing her face and hands.

She ran back to her room and went into the closet where she kept her list. The closet was huge, a walk-in that was the length of the room and about six feet wide. For a child with an imagination, this became a cave, a secret hiding place. To Carol as a new teenager, it offered privacy from the room she shared with her sister. An identical closet was on the other side of the room for her sister, so this closet was totally Carol's.

She pulled the string to turn on the overhead light and looked at her list, pasted to the wall inside her closet, as she glanced also at her watch.

6:30—get up, use bathroom, wash

6:33—get dressed, go down for breakfast

6:43—brush teeth

6:47—make bed

6:49—get books ready, comb hair

It was already 6:36, so she was off schedule because she didn't get up exactly at 6:30. Darn she thought. She had carefully planned her entire day, feeling virtuous and in control at the order and precision of her plans. Every minute of the day was assigned a task and Carol knew that if she could just stick to this schedule, life would be smoother, order would reign.

At school during study hall, she began charting out her evening, based on the amount of homework she had in each class. If she calculated everything accurately, she'd know exactly how much time she had to play after school, talk on the phone with friends, eat, watch TV and do homework. She had to be in bed by ten, so it was crucial to figure out how much time could be allotted to each activity this evening.

She thought about it, chewed the end of her pencil and continued writing. She realized the chart would change, depending on the amount of homework; so this would be a Monday to Friday schedule. Next she started plotting out the weekend.

When her weekly time schedule was neatly arranged, she turned her attention to the disorder inside herself. One of her teachers had accused her of having no self-control, because she laughed out loud during class at something a classmate whispered to her. Instead of dismissing it easily as another student would have done, Carol internalized this criticism and agonized over it. Did she really have no self control? She wrote self-control at the top of a clean page of paper and accepted (for the moment) that she had none. What was it exactly and how could she get it? She made a note to look it up at the library and then to take steps to attain it.

The second thing she wrote was "anger." The teacher really pissed her off when she criticized her in front of the whole class. "Carol, you have no self-control." Anger was a deadly thing to have, she knew, so she wrote under anger, "Get rid of it" and underlined it several times. Just how she planned to do that she wasn't sure, but there had to be a way to conquer this vice as well. She made a few notes on the things that made her angry, why she got angry and how to substitute another response when something made her angry.

She continued making a list of the things about herself that needed improvement. She looked with dismay as the list grew. I'm so far from perfection she thought, I'll never attain it in this lifetime. She closed her notebook as the bell rang signifying the end of study hall. One of her friends caught up with her and she smiled brightly as they began chatting about boys and the dance on Friday and biology lab. Carol guarded closely the things she wrote in her notebook. She didn't want any of her friends to know about her list, her introspection, her fears. She discussed these things with no one. How could she tell anyone that she thought she was so very different from everyone else? That she felt like a very flawed human being?

She was sure no one else had these kinds of thoughts, so she kept them to herself. Instead, she presented a cheerful face to everyone. To her friends she was the life of a party, always making jokes, and seeing the humor in all situations. She was sarcastic and funny and people enjoyed being around her. She was popular with boys as well as girls.

To her teachers, she was a bright student, but not really tested since schoolwork came very easily to her. She didn't study much and found high school, for the most part, boring. Her exuberance they saw as impudence. These were, after all, nuns in a strict Catholic school in the early 60s. The teachers had one view of her, her friends another, but Carol knew inside that neither really knew her. This was OK with her; she preferred hiding behind the masks she presented. She rather liked that she could control what people thought of her simply by presenting a certain mask. Even her close friends saw only parts of the real Carol. Many *thought* they knew her, but in fact, she was mostly unknown, sometimes, she feared, even to herself.

When she began reading Plato in college and came across his dictum, *Know Thyself*, she took up the challenge in a serious way. She knew she'd always been on this quest, but now it deserved greater attention. She came to the conclusion that it was a very difficult task to know oneself, but that it was a worthy pursuit if it led to self-improvement. She observed that most people were not concerned with knowing themselves, and that in fact, many people denied very basic things about themselves. She wanted to be free of this illusion by facing the negative qualities she had within and dealing with them.

Structure equals order; there must be some way to make order out of chaos, she thought, thinking of herself. If she rode herself hard enough, she could be a better person. If one is aiming for moral perfection, one must have self-discipline. This was her attempt to get it.

She was always willing to face herself, to face the worst things about herself and change them, if possible. More than anything, Carol wanted to be *good*.

*   *   *

Carol heard John moving around the room getting dressed, but she kept her eyes closed, wanting to retain the essence of the dream before it slipped away. Why did she dream of that memory of her adolescent 'lists'? Did she think her list-making was queer? She thought, of course, of the chapter she was working on of Franklin's self-improvement 'lists' and wondered if there was a connection here.

She heard John go downstairs so she stretched out on her back and pushed the pillow up behind her head, crossing her arms under it. What *is* this about, she ruminated, for she knew the coincidence of the dream meant something. She knew for sure that it was true *there were no coincidences*. With that in mind she began searching for the meaning.

Did Franklin's list of virtues denote vanity or humility? Historical opinion was divided on that, but many felt it came from a certain smugness. Carol did her inner checking, closing her eyes to get deeper into the subject. What did her own lists mean?

She thought of how she had felt such inner chaos as an adolescent. Looking back she saw that the lists were her unconscious mind's way of trying to put some order in her life. Her fears and anxieties may have gone out of control had it not been for the belief that the lists would help her get things under control. Smugness or superiority were about the last things she felt. And the lists had worked. At least for as long as she needed them.

She remembered when her sister found the list and cruelly made fun of her, running through the house reading 'Carol's crazy lists.' Carol was furious and in tears at this invasion of privacy and mockery of what was a serious project to her. As usual, their mother intervened and gave Carol back the papers and Mary was chided and told to not touch Carol's private things.

But it was ruined for Carol. If her sister found these lists so crazy and ridiculous, then perhaps they were. Her sense of order was gradually coming about as she got older and by the time she finished high school, she no longer used the lists.

She knew then, in an intuitive flash of awareness, that Franklin had likewise felt the same sense of disorderliness within himself, despite the exterior that the world saw. Only he knew his own self and the disarray that was his and what he hoped would be set right by his attempts to order himself. It was because he felt weak morally that he strove to master these things. This did not come from vanity, but from true humility. How could his motives be so misunderstood? Yes, it was diligent self-examination, but others saw it as sanctimonious vanity.

"They're wrong," Carol said out loud getting out of bed. "If he thought he was superior, why would he be so determined and methodical about trying to attain these virtues? Why a list?"

She got in the shower and her mind was at full throttle now, trying to resolve the problem. When I make a grocery list or a To Do list, why am I doing it? Does that make me smug? Only a fool would think that. I want to make sure I don't forget. Isn't that the purpose of a list?

I think Franklin is like a general welfare fund. Everyone draws from him, then resents him for being the source. Carol knew her mind was stretching this reasoning, but then, that's the way wild minds work.

Chapter 15

Women played a significant part in Benjamin Franklin's life...there's no getting away from that. His first female relationship was, of course, with his mother. Though there isn't a lot of material on this relationship, we do know that Ben always treated his mother with deference and respect.

*Her name was Abiah Folger and she was the second wife of Josiah Franklin. Together they had ten children, Benjamin being the third youngest child and the youngest son. The family had seventeen children (seven from Josiah's first marriage). She may not have been very intelligent, but from all evidence she was a good and loving mother, probably strict with her children and subservient to her husband, as the times dictated. She certainly had good health, having borne ten children and never sick in her life until she died at age eighty-five. Though his father appeared to be a more dominating influence on young Ben, his mother was always treated with respect and his detached kind of love. His letters to her have the tone of a dutiful son who is optimistic and reports only positive events, never wanting to cause her undue concern. When she died he was calm and accepting (Remember, he **always** took death well).*

His actual split with his family (which occurred when he ran away from home at age sixteen) was never really healed. With his famous detachment, he neither looked back in regret nor ever spoke ill of his parents.

The female he was closest to in his family was his youngest sister Jane Mecom. They were devoted to each other and corresponded regularly until his death. He gave Jane advice, money, support. Her life was as riddled with bad luck as his was with good, and he did everything he could to help her and her family.

Perhaps the sister and the mother set the tone for the way he treated other women in his life; that is, with care, offering guidance and companionship. Quite simply, he **liked** women, and despite (or perhaps because of) his flirtatious nature, he came across to most women as the caring uncle or father figure. Safely married to Deborah, he indulged this side of his personality, **always** having female friends which Deborah apparently found harmless.

On a trip to New England in 1754, he met Catharine Ray, a young woman less than half his age and perhaps he fell a tiny bit in love with her. Their letters are certainly flirtatious, slightly naughty, ("affectionately avuncular", biographer, Lopez says). It **could** have been a lust-like attraction on his part, but despite the temptation, he never succumbed (or, more accurately perhaps, she never succumbed.) He retained a lifelong affection and correspondence with her.

It is interesting to observe that when the flirtations were taken seriously by the women, he backed off, quickly referring to his wife and his happy domesticity. I believe he never intended for his propositions to be taken seriously and he was frightened when they were. It was the chase he enjoyed, with neither intention nor desire of a capture.

Another woman about whom there was serious speculation was Madame Brillon and this was when he moved to Paris in 1776. She was in her thirties when they met...he was seventy-one, suffering from gout, eczema, stones. Though their relationship was admittedly flirtatious, it was certainly not sexual. First of all, Madame Brillon called him Papa, an indication of the nature of her relationship with him. Further, he was friends with **Monsieur** Brillon...hardly the case if he had been sleeping with the wife. The flirting went on in front of the husband. Clearly, no one thought of Doctor Franklin as a lecher or a dirty old man (other than American history books and John Adams, whom I will discuss in a later chapter).

In fact, in a letter to him, Madame Brillon sums up his attraction to women, "I found in your letter, besides tokens of your friendship, a tinge of *that gaiety and that gallantry that cause all women to love you, because you love them all." (APS, XLIII, 30 from* **Mon Cher Papa,** *letter from Madame Brillon to BF.)*

If indeed Franklin had screwed around as much as history says he did, wouldn't there have been some irate husbands? After all, most of the women were married. Wouldn't he have made more enemies in Paris if he were that way? But noooo; they all loved him. Wouldn't there have been some written commentary on his licentiousness if it existed? Some breath of scandal? Wouldn't some woman have bragged of having seduced the famous Dr. Franklin? After all, he was a celebrity and everyone vied for his company and attentions.

There was none. Not a shred of evidence that he even had sex in France. His interest in women, I suggest, was not primarily sexual, but friendly, paternal, platonic.

In Paris, the other woman he spent a great deal of time with was Madame Helvetius, widow of the famed philosopher. She was in her late fifties when they met and he did indeed fall in love with her. Other than Deborah, this was the only woman he wanted to marry. She refused his proposal and he took it well. They remained friends until his death. Did they have an affair? As with any other woman in history, **there is no evidence to support this.**

But if they did, well, so what? He was a widower, she a widow (free, and over twenty-one as the saying goes). Why did she not marry him? She loved him, that much is clear. He would have gladly stayed there until his death, but around 1786, he felt an inner pull to go home and die in his homeland. The saddest, most poignant letter of his that I ever read, was the one written to her as his ship was about to sail for America.

"...I am not sure that I shall be happy in America, but I must go back. I feel sometimes that things are badly arranged in this world when I consider that people so well matched to be happy together are forced to separate.

"I will not tell you of my love. For one would say that there is nothing remarkable or praiseworthy about it, since everybody loves you. I only hope that you will always love me some....If I arrive in America, you shall soon hear

from me. I shall always love you. Think of me sometimes and write sometimes to your Benjamin Franklin." (Mon Cher Papa)

He was in his seventies during his years in Paris, and not in good health. Is it really probable that he was sexually active? Where is this lecher role that history assigned to Ben Franklin?

Women turned to him for glamour (he was a star); and amusement (enormously witty, conversational and well informed); as well as for guidance and comfort (he was wise, sincere and caring). It's significant to note that all the commentary about Franklin being a womanizer was started by men.

His appreciation for women was expressed likewise in his writing. His first pen name was a woman, Silence Dogood, whose letters were impudent and clever. In the fourteen letters he wrote in her name, he made fun of women's fashions (hoopskirts) and their discomfort to women; pleaded for freedom of speech, education for girls; and he suggested compensation insurance for widows and spinsters. This (remember) is a sixteen-year old boy speaking! Does it sound to you the way it does to me? A young man ahead of his time championing the rights of women? He often took female pen names (anonymous writing was a lifelong habit of his) to express the feminine side of himself that was evident and that he was not at all ashamed to admit.

"Always a person himself, Franklin treated every woman as if she were a person too, and made her feel more truly one than ever. Because he loved, valued, and studied women, they were no mystery to him, and he had no instinctive fear of them." (Van Doren p. 653)

Friendships with women were easier and humorous, without artifice and jealousies (unlike with men such as Adams, Deane and Jay for example). Gallantry came naturally to him, and women responded because unlike the majority of eighteenth century men, Franklin genuinely liked them as people. He valued women's intuition over reason. His admiration for women was genuine; how could any woman not respond to this? Undoubtedly he **could** have taken advantage of this simpatico and seduced many women he befriended. But did he?

Apart from other men's jealousies, there is little real evidence to support the tradition of Franklin as a lecher. Sorry, Mr. Adams.

Chapter 16

Carol's affair nearly destroyed their marriage, though on the surface it appeared to cause barely a ripple.

Daniel Barton, respected and well-known authority on structural linguistics from the University of Southampton in England, was enticed to come to Bodley for a semester as visiting professor. His book on structural linguistics was a landmark work that had become the standard text for graduate studies in that field. Carol was thrilled that he accepted the invitation to teach and lecture. The amount of money Carol had pressured the committee into offering him had something to do with it. Carol, as his sponsoring faculty member, would undoubtedly have to spend a great deal of time with him.

She guessed she expected a bookish, ordinary man, and was surprised to find him extraordinarily handsome and, like her, in his late thirties. He was tall and muscular with thick black hair and a beard and he was not married. His eyes were lively and his sense of humor was earthy. Carol was attracted to him immediately.

He arrived in the middle of August and his first weekend there, she invited him to the house where she and John hosted a cookout for him to meet other colleagues. He was a success with the men as well as with the women because he was brilliant and handsome, with a hint of the rogue.

Carol shared her office with him since her regular office mate was on sabbatical. Their comfort with each other grew as they got to know each other.

Often he came to the house where John was a gracious host; but with linguistics being a popular topic, John often found himself excluded. On one occasion, feeling impatient with the two-way conversation, he excused himself, saying he had work to do in his study. Carol was relieved he'd gone, for she was concerned that he would notice the element of flirtatiousness that had lately become part of her interchanges with Daniel. Alone, she gave into it a little more freely. Nothing overt was said, mostly it was innuendo and eye contact. Still, it was an undercurrent that both of them were aware of.

One Friday afternoon as they sat in their office, the air conditioner died. It had been a very hot and humid autumn day.

"Oh, that's just great," Carol said, pushing a lock of her blond hair off her forehead. "It'll be like a sauna in here in minutes."

Daniel laughed and said Americans seem to tolerate extremes of weather less than other cultures.

"You're full of shit," she replied good-naturedly. "The human body temperature is 98.6 no matter where one lives, and hot is hot."

"What about that lake you were telling me about? Could we go for a swim?"

"I...don't have a suit with me," she said.

"Neither do I," he said with an exaggerated leer.

Carol felt her face get hot. She'd been married nine years and though there always were temptations and attractions to other men, she didn't take them too seriously, valuing John and her marriage. She never thought of herself as the kind of woman who would cheat on her husband. With Daniel, she felt such a stirring of desire that she kept inching closer, not wanting to give in to the attraction but not wanting to give it up either. She knew she was playing with fire. She also knew he was attracted to her and wanted to take the attraction further.

"It really is hot. Let's go."

They locked the office and got into his car and she directed him to the lake via back roads. She knew a secluded area that was private and hidden by trees, where she and John had often gone swimming. As they drove along, her hair blowing in the wind of the open window, this handsome, sexy man by her side, Carol deliberately blocked out John and decided to enjoy the moment and the company. She wasn't doing anything wrong, she reasoned. For godsakes we're only going swimming.

She showed him the narrow dirt road that steeped slightly as it wound further into the woods toward the lake. When the path narrowed, they left the car and walked the rest of the way. He had a blanket in his car and they spread it on the sandy, rocky clearing by the lake.

"This is very private," he said, his voice sounding like a whisper. Birds and gnats made their noises and far off the motor of a boat could be heard, but all around them was silence.

"C'mon, the water looks ready." She ducked behind a bush and removed everything but her bra and underpants. He stripped down to his jockey shorts and they entered the lake, slipping quickly under the water.

"God, this feels great," he said swimming with great strokes away from shore. She doggie-paddled, keeping only her head above water, until he was farther away from her, then swam in another direction. They swam and enjoyed the cool refreshing water for about forty-five minutes, gradually floating closer to each other and chatting amiably. Carol wasn't sure how to get out of the water without him seeing her, so she asked him to turn away while she got out.

"Such modesty," he said playfully, but he took a deep breath and quickly disappeared below the surface. As Carol turned toward shore, she felt something grab her ankles and lift her up, tossing her backward into the water.

"You rat," she screamed as she regained her footing.

He was laughing hard watching her sputter. She hit her palms against the water splashing him in the face as he tried to hold his hands up in defense. Now she was laughing. He swam toward her and grabbed her hands to stop her.

"There now, enough of that," he said holding her wrists by her sides. Suddenly conscious of each other, they stopped laughing and the sound of their breathing was the only sound. His body was close and she was achingly aware of the thick black hair on his chest, his beard dripping water and his eyes making no secret about what he was feeling. The tops of her breasts broke the surface of the water and without taking his eyes from hers, his hands reached up and started pulling the bra straps down her arms. He did this so slowly, giving her a chance to stop him if she were going to, that Carol was practically limp with desire. He slowly brought his mouth to hers and with a moan, she wrapped her arms around him as he lifted her up and carried her effortlessly out of the water and onto the blanket.

The ground was hard on her back, but she knew she would have hardly noticed if she were lying on broken glass at that point. She saw the sun through the trees and the heard the sound of the water lapping as his body moved strong and sure on hers. Then the world was blocked out in a blinding, roaring explosion that removed everything except the acute awareness of this man in her arms, his body pressing itself into hers.

He didn't move for a long time. Her lips tasted the salty dampness of his shoulder and she licked it. He shuddered with pleasure and kissed her hair, then slowly drew his face back to look at her. His eyes were as intense and smoky as hers and they looked deeply into each other, neither regretting what had occurred.

Later he dropped her back at her car in the faculty parking lot. She slid behind the wheel and opened all the windows; the car was stuffy with heat. She rummaged in her bag and found a comb, pulling it through her nearly dry hair. Her face was suffused with color and her eyes looked wild. What would John see, she worried.

She drove home and the closer she got to home, the more the enormity of what she'd done hit her. She'd cheated on her husband, she'd broken her marriage vows. The passion cooled, she felt an overwhelming sense of loss and regret.

She let herself in and the coolness of her house's interior was like a rebuke, and a refuge. Suddenly her knees gave out and she sank to the floor, her briefcase still in her hand. She lay, face down, arms and legs spread out like a fallen snow angel, her face against the cool marble floor of the foyer. She heard John's footsteps coming in from the kitchen.

"Well, well, what's this? Did someone have a bad day?" He sat on the floor next to her and stroked her head. She kept her eyes tightly shut, unable to look at him. Her voice was tight as she whispered, "Yes."

"I think I have the antidote for that." His voice was gentle and soothing as he talked about the cool vegetable salad and icy white wine he had ready for her. Carol could feel the heat and the madness of her afternoon receding as John's calm voice soothed her. She stretched out a finger and gently touched his knee. He had on khaki shorts and sandals and she let her hand rest against the soft hair on his legs. She was fighting the urge to cry and dreaded John seeing that.

"Here, why don't you take a shower and lie down for awhile. We can eat later." He picked up her briefcase and put it in her office and Carol took his advice and went upstairs.

Chapter 17

When she saw Daniel on Monday at school she was going to tell him they had to forget what happened. He was on the phone and his voice faltered in the conversation as she walked into the office. When he finished he turned and looked at her, his eyes warm and yet watchful.

"How are you?"

"I'm OK." She busied herself with papers on her desk and avoided looking at him.

"Carol." He said just her name and his tone forced her to look at him as she stood by her desk, papers in her hands.

"I'm in great danger of falling in love with you." He made it sound like a joke, but his eyes were serious.

"Don't, Daniel. What happened Friday was...a mistake. I can't continue anything...you know...John."

"Go back to where we were before? Just like that?"

"Yes, that's it," she shuffled papers. "Go back to where we were before."

And so for awhile they tried to resume the casualness of their former relationship. But one night at a party, John was in another room and they suddenly found themselves alone on a dark patio. Maybe because they'd had several glasses of wine, he reached over and stroked her bare upper arm and desire raced through her like wildfire.

The next morning, Sunday, Carol told John she had to get something from her office and went to campus. She let herself in and shortly thereafter, Daniel arrived. They locked the door.

The affair continued sporadically for the rest of the semester, and somewhere along the way, though they were extremely discreet and truly believed no one knew, John found out. She had more evening classes and meetings and appointments that soon even John grew suspicious and his heart filled with dread.

One evening in December it was snowing and Carol was getting ready to leave to meet Daniel at his apartment.

"You're going out on a night like this?" John asked from the easy chair in the living room as she put her coat on. He lowered the newspaper and watched her. "It's snowing like crazy."

"I told you I have to get a few things from the library."

"Can't it wait until tomorrow?" His voice was reasonable, the question was reasonable.

"No, it can't wait." Their eyes met as she pulled a scarf around her head. In that moment a transmission passed between them. She knew John knew and an acknowledgement of what the other knew was recognized.

It was snowing worse than she thought. Snow was drifting and visibility was practically nil. Her affair with Daniel was clouding her judgement. This was stupid, out driving on a night like this. No other cars were on the road and her headlights played over the growing mounds of snow. Snow plows were on the main roads spreading sand and salt. She drove slowly, still determined to get to Daniel's. Her lust for him had not abated. She knew she wasn't in love with him, nor he with her, though for awhile she thought she was. It was just this powerful, physical attraction and the joy of forbidden sex. They'd gotten a little careless, unable to stay apart for more than a few days, but tonight, knowing John knew was a shock.

Still, because she wasn't thinking clearly, she didn't consider all the ramifications of this new knowledge. Maybe I'm wrong; maybe he doesn't know, she tried to convince herself.

She turned a corner and though she was going slowly, there was absolutely no traction on the road and her car slid sideways. She braked and tried to steer into the turn, but the car was out of control. It slid silently and deliberately into a snowdrift. She took a deep breath and tried to stay calm. She put the car in reverse and tried to back it out, but it was too slippery for the tires to get any traction. They spun the car a little more securely into the bank.

"Damn." She sat helplessly for a moment thinking about what to do. It occurred to her, for she wasn't a dense person, that what was happening to her now was a waking dream. She'd been out driving where she shouldn't be going, betraying John. She knew the metaphoric road she was traveling was dangerous and now the inevitable happened. She was stuck, in trouble and couldn't get out. Is this what she wanted?

The unseen world of guidance was trying to tell her something. She believed this was often the way life guided her, and she could either get the message or go on the way she was going, out of control on this dangerous road.

She suddenly felt cold, and it wasn't just from the temperature. After the first time she'd made love with Daniel, she vowed to end it right there. Instead, she had thrown caution and good sense to the wind and turned deaf ears to the voice of reason within her. She *wanted* him and so she put John and marriage in the back of her mind while she slept with Daniel.

She sat in her car staring at the pile of snow in front of her, on her hood, trapping her, and she knew it was really over. She could not possibly continue this madness with Daniel and still face John another day. The alternative was not even a possibility.

Feeling like she'd been thrown out of a prison...one of her own making to be sure...she got out, locked the car and leaving it in the drift, walked home.

"You were right, it was crazy going out tonight," she told John when she got home a half hour later, practically frozen. He looked at her, unreadable and said nothing.

Nor did he say anything when the next day they went to get her car and it was in the opposite direction from the campus.

Chapter 18

Carol's lust had gotten her into trouble once before. When she was seventeen, she was madly in love with her high school boyfriend, Jim. No boy's kisses had ever made her want more...until Jim's. These were new feelings for her, these yearnings and desires and she wanted to give into them.

Boyfriend Jim was afraid to go further. In the early 60s, fear of disease was not the big passion-killer, pregnancy was. Both had been brought up with religion and fear; Carol was just more willing to let hers go.

They petted and necked and steamed up the inside of the car windows parked under trees in out of the way places, and made themselves stop before going "all the way."

It was inevitable that the boy would eventually find it impossible to resist the girl, especially since she was so willing.

Their worst fears were justified...Carol got pregnant. They discussed getting married but knew they were too young. They were both terrified of telling their parents. The alternative was abortion.

Jim found the money, Carol found the doctor and the deed was done.

The whole experience made them sad, sobered, and fearful of any more sex. When they parted for different colleges, they promised to stay in touch, stay in love, but it was already over and they both knew it.

Later, when Carol reflected on it, she took the blame for what happened. Jim had been willing to wait until they were older and could get married, but Carol was too eager for the sensations that her body promised. She knew she tempted him beyond endurance.

At college, she promptly went on the pill. Sex was too enjoyable to give up. At first she felt she was doing something slightly naughty, but as her life philosophy formed, she came to believe that sex was natural and meant to be enjoyed. It didn't control her life; she was from an early age, a woman of moderation and balance in all things, but she did give it a prominent place in her list of things that made life worthwhile.

Discreet and careful about whom she had sex with, she found, after a while, that it was best when you loved the person. There was one serious love affair during college and when that ended, Carol decided to put her energies into other things and she started graduate school. She came to the conclusion that she was oversexed and that she needed to work on that moral imperfection. She would be celibate until she fell in love again, and so she was until she met John.

When she had what she thought of as an epiphany that night stuck in the snow, she knew that the same demon that got her when she was seventeen got her again at thirty-seven: she let her body make a decision that should have been in the jurisdiction of her mind...or better yet, her heart.

When she made a decision, or a mistake, she rarely looked back in regret or recrimination. She let it go and moved on. Thus, when she informed Daniel on the Monday after the snow incident, that their affair was truly over, she had already moved herself beyond it. He was hurt and confused by her abruptness and her chill and tried to argue with her but she was immovable. She moved her things to another office until after he was gone for good. The semester was nearly over and she saw the symbolism of that coincidence.

She was ashamed of what had happened, mostly for the cost to John, but also because it showed her her own character weakness. She prided herself on being a stronger person morally; now she had to face her failure in this area. Her usual attitude of What's done is done, let's get on with life, sustained her own sense of self, and since John didn't bring it up, she assumed (wrongly) that he shared this approach. John never accused her, so taking her cue from him she decided not to mention it either. She hoped that perhaps they could both just let it go and move beyond it.

Unfortunately, she didn't understand that John needed more than that. He wanted her remorse but from her outer appearances, she didn't have any.

Chapter 19

"It doesn't take much to make an enemy;
with some all you have to do is disagree."

Ben Franklin to Carol Byrd,
April, 1988

Carol spread the papers out around her, working on the chapter about his detractors. She looked at her notes describing the variety of criticism leveled at him from his early days to the present. It was unbelievable to her that 200 years after his death, there still were critical attacks on Ben Franklin.

The negative criticism is niggling, Carol decided and overwhelmingly in the minority. She wished she had the space in this book (and the time) to demolish all of them, swiftly and succinctly with her saber words, but most of the offenders were dead and she didn't know who it would be for.

In all of them she noted the same recognizable strand of jealousy that permeated most of the criticism.

John Adams. How kind was history to him? OK, so he was a president (read politician). Based on her latest readings, Carol now viewed him as a hypocritical, uptight, prig; judgmental and self-serving...but then, weren't most politicians? Isn't he really just true to form? And since he was one of the first, mayhap he is a model for the politician state-of-consciousness. On an ethics scale, she thought, the archetype is on a par with a used car salesman.

Adams and his wife, the famous Abigail, were very proper people who were critical not only of Ben, but of people like him. They felt he was a threat to good, moral, God-fearing folks, (such as themselves). Carol compared them mentally to the current right wing, pro-life groups, the Phyllis Schlaflys or self-righteous religious groups who sanctimoniously try to force their beliefs on everyone, believing (by some moral delusion) that their beliefs are superior and in fact, the only right ones. The whole world, therefore, should believe as they do.

John Adams gave slight recognition to Franklin's skills as a statesman, denigrated his position as a scientist and made personal attacks whenever possible. He wrote a scathing and contemptuous comment about Franklin dozing off during the 1787 Continental Congress. (*For chrissakes, John, he was 81 years old and in poor health, and probably bored by your pomposity.*) She sneered this rebuke to the ghost of John Adams.

What was clear to Carol, and perhaps to other historians (for there was ample support for her theory,) is that John Adams was jealous of Franklin. Pure and simple. People admired Franklin and he was the recipient of widespread adulation. The French positively *loved* him, which rankled Adams to no end. Franklin, Adams and Silas Deane were the committee sent to negotiate with the French. The French however, refused to deal with anyone but Franklin. When Adams wrote home about Franklin, he was positively splenetic; a petty person who would attempt to diminish Franklin in everyone's eyes, even the government he was representing in France.

Fortunately, Franklin's reputation as a loyal and brilliant ambassador was solid, and Adams' nasty letter home from France was mostly regarded as sour grapes.

Go make wine, Abigail.

Incredibly, Adams stated that he believed Franklin caused the French Revolution. That's a pretty powerful feat for one who, according to Adams, was deficit in so many virtues.

Carol dismissed Adams' criticism pretty much as history had. There will always be men, Carol observed, who in the face of greater men, will attempt to destroy what they themselves cannot be. It stems from the lowliest of motives...jealousy.

She picked up her notes on D. H. Lawrence. The viciousness of his attack was rather interesting. It's not as though he lived in the same time as Franklin...or did he, she thought? Wouldn't that be an interesting twist? Adams reincarnates as D. H. Lawrence. She put that aside as a pleasant whimsy to contemplate later and looked instead at the words. Of the two, she didn't know who was more vitriolic.

What would make an English writer, writing over a hundred and thirty years after the death of a certain American, hate him? What did Benjamin Franklin ever do to him to warrant such a personal attack?

Carol caught herself reacting in a human way rather than as an objective historian. She thought briefly of her own dislike for Lawrence which was in place long before she even thought about Franklin. She had read Lawrence thoroughly, of course, (should one ever criticize anything one does not know?) and thought his prose and his life view rather tortured and convoluted and extremely dark. It was not especially satisfying to her to read his cheerless prose.

But it was Lawrence's comments on Franklin's soul that intrigued. For godsakes, she thought impatiently, what right did Lawrence have to comment on another's soul? Isn't that between the Soul and God? What audacity! What ego! What impertinence!

She laughed inwardly at her thoughts. Listen to me, taking umbrage with DH as though Franklin were my personal charge. The human consciousness is so incredibly amusing...even my own.

It was clear that Lawrence had not read Franklin carefully and what he had read he didn't understand. He zeroed in, with a limited perception, on Franklin's morality and this became his banner. He despised Franklin's morality. *Jeez, David Herbert, I'm not a shrink, but something is pretty obvious here.*

Lawrence talked about Franklin's soul being shoddy and cheap...trite! (How dare he?) Whereas his soul was like a dark forest. (this is better?) Lawrence refers to his soul as a dark forest several times in his now famous, defamatory essay.

Just because you are a dark forest, David Herbert, doesn't mean all souls are. Your atavism has obscured your perceptions.

Lawrence's sexuality was always an issue for him, a hang-up that was reflected in everything he wrote. Franklin, on the other hand, clearly enjoyed his sexuality with none of the post-Victorian inhibitions that possessed Lawrence.

Carol was so involved in the text she was writing that she missed the subtle change in atmosphere that denoted his presence.

"Ahem. Must you be so hard on Mr. Lawrence?"

She turned quickly, startled. "Oh, hello. Yes, in fact, I must. Don't you agree?"

Amused, he pulled up a chair next to her and read from her page: 'Lawrence's vitriol is as nasty as a dose of liver oil and one can only hope that for him it had the same effect: purgative.' Carol, really."

She sniffed, took the page and folded it in half, her way of discarding it. "Very well, I won't use that particular sentence. But on the whole, yes, I intend to be hard on him. Do you really not agree?"

"Your defense is charming, but are you not doing exactly what he did? Attacking the personal?"

"But don't you see, he's pointing out things about you that are really things wrong with him? He camouflages his personal attack—or tries to—by saying it's your morals he objects to. But his whole essay really says more about him and his aberrations than it does about you. I think he's uncomfortable with his own morality."

"Exactly. His criticism of me forced you to look at him. Isn't that always the way it is? It has always been my observation that when one spews forth venom about another, it is most telling about the individual doing the spewing." He smiled at her mischievously. "Poor Richard might say, 'what goes round comes round.' A wiser philosopher said, 'You can't recognize something in another unless it exists within yourself.'"

She was quiet a moment. "I know you're right, Ben. It's just this urge to defend or retaliate against his nastiness."

"Resist it; don't fall into that trap." He was firm and she felt somewhat chastised. He didn't communicate again and soon Carol was absorbed in her work and forgot about him.

Why is it certain figures in history draw or repel us? Why should any-one—centuries removed—care about the personality or personal life of someone who lived in the past? What business is it of ours? Carol sat in her darkening study, her feet propped on her desk thinking about this. She was about to turn the desk light on to begin writing, but instead let these thoughts have free rein within her head, to see where it would lead.

Ben said it is never more than a mirror image when we like or dislike a person. The world is always reflecting back to us images of our own self. Can it be any other way? That we can only recognize something in others if it exists in ourselves? It wasn't an entirely new thought to Carol when he said it, but it rang as Truth.

Carol thought about how people gossip about others. Are all the unkind things really the speaker's garbage and not the person being gos-siped about? Or do they belong to both? How can you recognize greed unless you've experienced the feeling? Or anger? Or anything? And how do you know it? Ah, it exists (or, be generous to yourself, it has existed) within you.

A mirror can only reflect what we know. Otherwise the image makes no impression at all.

She picked up a pen and jotted a few more lines. *Sorry, but back to D. H. Lawrence. What he saw as inferior morality in Franklin was only a reflection of his own confused and possibly dark morality. (Dark is a word he hearkens to spiritually; it is not a criticism I am leveling.)*

John Adams, an uptight, sexually frustrated prig. He saw Franklin as lech-erous; but he, Adams, admitted that from an early age he had a weakness for the female form. He, however, (do we hear sanctimony?) fought it. Did not give into it, would not. (What festering that must have caused within you, Mr. Adams, this denial of what is so very human.)

Well, well, well, Mr. President. What is the world mirror showing you?

Franklin, on the other hand, was unremittingly kind to others, and despite the criticism and vociferous expression of dislike by his enemies, he was never known to retaliate in kind; never said anything unkind about them.

Well! Surely the world mirrored for him as well.

Carol thought of how she could apply this new insight to her own life. If all the world's a mirror, then what is she seeing? And what of John's outlook? He was patient and accepting and much more tolerant of others than she. He saw good in others; Carol was more cynical than he. But then, she thought fondly, John is a good person.

As if on cue, he knocked on her door and walked in.

"Hello. Any reason for sitting in the dark?"

"Oh, hi. Just thinking."

"Profound stuff?" he leaned down putting his hands on her shoulders.

She tilted her head back to look at him upside down. "About you actually. I was thinking what a good person you are."

"Well, I thank you for the compliment," he said softly, leaning down to kiss her.

She put her feet down on the floor and sat up straight, turning her desk light on.

John picked up a paper with a quote on it and read it out loud, "'The variety of his character has made it possible to praise and damn him with equal vigor.' Hmm that's interesting; who said this?"

She flipped a four by six index card and looked at it. "Someone named John W. Ward; it's from an essay he wrote."

"You're researching his enemies?"

"It fascinates me that he had them. I can't find anything to dislike about this guy."

"Whoa," John said putting the card down and drawing back to look at her. "I thought you were looking for his manly, mortal flaws...you're saying he doesn't have any?"

"No, don't be silly," she said getting up and turning off the desk light. "No one's perfect; I'm just finding he's one of the good guys. Like you," she tiptoed and kissed him on the mouth.

Chapter 20

Notes:

The thing that really bugs me about his detractors is the nit-picking they do in an attempt to denigrate him. When a jealous person is trying to turn others against his object of hatred, he will stretch the truth to make a case. Or lie outright. Or resort to name calling.

Is any of this worthy of scholarly writing? Where is academic, intellectual fairness?

Lawrence calls Franklin (four times in his infamous essay) "snuff-colored." What exactly does that mean anyway? Is it an insult, and if so why? Can someone do something about the color of one's skin, if indeed this is what Lawrence was talking about? What kind of imbecilic criticism is this? Snuff-colored for chrissakes! Shall we say you were pasty colored with sunken cheeks and an embarrassing beard, David Herbert? Would that be valid criticism of you? What kind of intellectual are you who would include that kind of nasty commentary in a critical essay (for godsakes)?

Critics of Lawrence's criticism of Franklin offer this:

-. *Lawrence confused the writer with the character of the Autobiography, since the Autobiography is DHL's source.*

-. *Lawrence did not understand Franklin*

-. *Lawrence overlooks Franklin's self-deprecating humor*

-. Lawrence has limited perception; clearly he has not read Franklin carefully or thoroughly.

-. Toward the end of the essay, Lawrence is positively irrational.

Why was this essay ever taken seriously or given any credence? Why is it referenced so often? Lawrence has stature as a novelist, (surely even I won't argue that), but as a critic of BF, where does he stand?

Further, he accused Franklin of having "no concern, really, with the immortal Soul." The reason? He was "too busy being social." Let me address the second point, David Herbert, by referring you to the chapter on the list of inventions and accomplishments that Franklin was responsible for in his 84 years. Would you care to match your lifetime of accomplishment against his? What were you too busy doing? Nuff said. (or should I say 'snuff said?')

About Soul...jeez, this is really touchy, and rather tawdry of you I might add. What kind of person would have the audacity (or ego) to presume to comment on another's private, innermost, intangible facet of themselves? Surely this domain is between Soul and God?

Lawrence argues we can never know our selves (our soul) because it is "a vast forest, a dark forest...with wild life in it." If you can't even know yourself, Mr. Lawrence, why would you dare to think you could know the state of Franklin's 'soul'?

Franklin said one of the hardest things to do is to know thyself. Lawrence said it is impossible. (I think there's a seed here for an article on the can-do spirit.) Can we ever accomplish a deed after stating emphatically that it is impossible? Do you not first have to believe you can do something before you can do it? Lawrence said we can't know ourselves. Franklin spent his life trying to know himself.

A biblical dictum (presumably words from the Almighty): "Before you can know me, you must know thyself."

All right, let me lay off Lawrence. The only honest thing I found in Lawrence's essay on Franklin was this line: "I do not like him." Fair enough; I just wish he had spared me his reasons.

Is this critical discussion, critical inquiry, or academic nit-picking? Lawrence attacks Franklin, then critics for fifty plus years argue over his criticism?

*   *   *

John Adams. What can one say about a man who wanted to be called "Highness" instead of president? (I'm serious!) Very pompous, very concerned with himself. Petty, spiteful. He attacked William Franklin's "illegitimacy," by saying that electing this base born brat to the office of Governor (New Jersey) was an insult to the morals of America etceteras. Imagine William's humiliation (Adams did this publicly); imagine what kind of person Adams was to do this. What a slimeball!

As a young lawyer, Adams tried (in vain) to close all the public houses in Braintree, Massachusetts. He believed he knew what was best for everyone in Braintree…no drinking. I wonder if Abigail put him up to this? Nah, they were probably in agreement.

Adams was not in control of his temper. He thumped his cane on the floor at the Continental Congress. When he was defeated in anything, he yelled, sent indiscreet letters to his enemies, whined to his wife. .

This is funny: he accused Franklin of breaking out in a passion and swearing, contrary to his usual reserve. This is such an absurd accusation. He really must have been looking in his mirror that day.

He was nasty. In France, he accused Franklin of indolence. Let's remember, at this time Franklin was old, suffering from painful gout, chronic skin disease, swollen joints, achy feet, and eye fatigue. What exactly did Adams want Franklin to do? Why was he so nasty?

Another critic, Mark Twain. Well, his criticism is neither as vitriolic as Lawrence's nor as inflammatory. It is not that it is indefensible, but dismissable. Twain scorned Franklin's "stove" his "flying kite" and his fooling away of time when he ought to have been "foraging for soap fat, or constructing candles." Surely he is not serious. Twain was after all, a humorist. These criticisms are kind of funny. Without comment, therefore, I will say nothing further about Twain. Dismissed, sir, you missed the mark. (Get it? mark?)

Carol reread these preliminary notes and smiled to herself. It won't do, I know, but it felt good to write it anyway.

OK, let me be serious about D. H. Lawrence. He is one of those major literary figures with an aberrant psychology that is the cause of his being a great writer. His atavistic impulses to explore his own dark interior (as described by him 'a wild dark forest') are not normal. But it's OK. Without his atavism he could not have written **Sons and Lovers.** *Without it there would be no* **Lady Chatterly's Lover** *or* **The Rainbow.** *I'm not quibbling with his dark interior…he's most welcome to it. I'm trying to understand why he hated Franklin.*

I see this: he criticized what he could not be, which bespeaks an envy. He tried to be a soldier in World War I but was declared unfit for service. After that he was virulently critical of the war.

In England in the early twentieth century, class distinctions were difficult if not impossible to transcend. (I venture a speculation that it hasn't changed that much. Any country based on monarchy which infers that some people are born blessed by God and others are not is setting up an impossible class standard.) Lawrence was from the lower, working class. His parents, (father a coal miner and his mother an ex-school teacher), were ill-suited. They quarreled constantly and David developed a passionate attachment to his mother (file this under aberrant psychology beginnings.)

So the class thing, like the soldier thing, became issues for him. How does one overcome insecurities and inferiorities based on one's social status at birth?

By contrast we have a man like Benjamin Franklin, born in a country devoid of true class distinctions (at least in the early 18th century.) Like Lawrence, Franklin came from poor, peasant stock.

Aside from the sheer volume of Franklin's achievements, I suspect Lawrence was jealous of mainly one thing: **Franklin transcended his lower class roots.**

In his life, Franklin dined with kings, consorted with the most intellectually and socially elite of his day, was respected by scientists and was on equal footing with heads of state. He was honored and revered worldwide and nearly worshiped by the French. His company was sought after for his good humor, intellect, and charm.

In his own *Autobiographical Sketch*, Lawrence says, "As a man from the working class, I feel that the middle class cut off some of my vital vibration...I cannot make the transfer from my own class into the middle class."

With the greatest of ease, Franklin did.

Lawrence, by his own admission, never felt truly friendly with his fellow man, never felt successful as a human. Franklin, by anyone's standards, was the epitome of a successful human.

Such a simple, human thing: jealousy.

D. H. Lawrence wrote his essay on Franklin immediately after his first visit to America in 1923.

Chapter 21

There was a moment when I liked D. H. Lawrence. It occurred when I was reading his poem, "The Snake." In the beginning of the poem I did not like his images. Then in the middle of the poem when he felt honored by the snake's presence, my heart leaned toward him in understanding and empathy. It was as though he was recognizing the snake as Soul, a fellow creature of God, and for that reason it deserved to be honored. In that line and for that instant, there was truth. In the next verse, when he admits his fear, I am still with him.

At the end, he throws a log at the snake as his fear, revulsion and superiority get the better of him.

Yes, David, you have a pettiness to expiate.

Chapter 22

John was relieved when Daniel returned to England. The semester, as well as the affair, was over and he would no longer have to see Daniel and wonder if he was sleeping with Carol. He tried to tell himself that it had never really been an affair, just a flirtation, but he knew he was just denying the truth. His mind played with it until he was tormented and raging. Then, alternately he would fall into a deep sorrow over it and express his feelings in morbid poetry which he kept locked in a desk drawer. It never occurred to him to confront Carol and make demands or accusations. It was just not in him to do that.

Throughout it all, Carol remained in calm and stoic control. She and John had always been so very civilized that it was almost impossible for them to discuss it. She deeply regretted the affair and the pain it must have caused John, but he appeared to not want to discuss it; just go on as though nothing had happened. This was fine with her, for in a way she had moved beyond it. Once she made the decision to end it, she put Daniel out of her mind. Her life with John resumed as before and though there was an artificial politeness between them, they maintained appearances, not only in public, but when they were alone together as well. If they didn't talk as much when they were together, well, that was understandable, she thought. They'd been married for ten years, silences were to be expected.

The first time they went to bed together after the affair ended, was a failure. John was unable to sustain an erection and mumbled an excuse about being tired. Carol assured him that was fine. The next time was after they'd been to a party where he drank quite a bit. The sex was rough and selfish and Carol bit her lip and said nothing and began to wonder if this behavior was connected to her affair. After that, sex was infrequent and perfunctory.

John's manner toward her gradually began changing. Though he never confronted her directly, he began punishing her in subtle and almost unconscious ways: withholding sex when he knew she wanted it, making plans without her, being inconsiderate of her in small ways, picking petty fights when she was under stress for a deadline or project. At first she didn't see the pattern, and then she did.

For her part, when she realized how deeply she had hurt John and how damaging to their marriage the affair was, she suffered great remorse, which she was unable to express to John. She deeply regretted her lapse into lust and betrayal of her vows, for she knew it was lust only. She berated herself for being oversexed and immoral. When she resolved to end the affair, she also resolved never again to succumb to those base desires and to make it up to John by being a good wife. She would subvert any errant sexual desires into her work. She knew from over the years that John's need for sex was less than hers. He seemed satisfied if they made love once a week; Carol would have liked it more often. Since the affair, their intimacy, as well as their marriage, seemed to be crumbling.

One night, about six months after the affair ended, Carol was late getting home. It was after nine and John knew she'd been in a meeting. It was their unwritten rule that when one of them worked late the other would fix a plate and have it ready to pop into the microwave. She came in and threw her briefcase down and went into the living room.

"Hi," she said to John who was sitting in front of the TV in a recliner, legs stretched out.

"Hi," he answered barely looking up from the screen. She waited a moment, and then went into the kitchen. She looked in the refrigerator and didn't see a plate.

"What's for dinner?" she called into him. He didn't answer and she pushed the swinging door into the other room. "I didn't have dinner, did you make anything?"

He glanced at her and back to the TV. "I did, but there wasn't any left-over." She looked at him for a moment and then went back to the kitchen, slamming the door behind her.

It wasn't that big a deal, him not fixing dinner, but it was the final thing in a stress-filled day. The situation between them was becoming intolerable, and she felt hot, angry tears fill her eyes. She looked in the refrigerator for a moment then realized she was too angry to eat. She drank a glass of milk and took an aspirin, but she felt the rage and the frustration building. They were not violent people and they did not normally fight, but this was the end of the rope for her.

She knew she should calm down before she spoke to him, but the desire to lash out in her pain was too strong and she felt at the mercy of her anger.

She went into the room and stood in front of the TV, reaching to turn it off.

"Hey, I'm watching that."

He saw her eyes flashing danger but her voice was ice cold.

"I'm going to ask you a question and I want you to tell me the truth." She paused and took a deep breath. "Do you want to stay married or do you want out?"

"What the hell are you talking about?" His face paled.

Her voice was shaky and she spoke slowly through clenched teeth.

"I can't undo what I've done and I am sorrier than you will ever know. We can either try to repair the damage that I caused or we can call it quits. But I can't go on living this way." Her voice cracked and she bit her lip as she stared at him. He stared back, incredulous. This was the closest she'd come to admitting she'd had an affair and he wasn't sure he wanted to hear it; he didn't want her to say another word. Putting it into words would make it visual to him...real. Nameless, it remained an invisible thorn in their marriage, but he thought he could live with that. Maybe he was wrong. Either way it felt like hell.

She was staring at him, waiting. He stared back, unable to speak, caught off guard with this ultimatum. Yes, he knew he'd been playing games with her, deliberately trying to hurt her...not the way she'd hurt him, but still, it was a game. He couldn't believe she was forcing a show-down to a situation he felt was unresolvable.

Suddenly she seemed to deflate, the anger gone as he saw a flash of pain in her eyes.

"Let me know when you've made your decision," she said, barely audible and ran out of the room.

She showered and crawled into bed, tired and feeling almost sick. She wanted to cry but something inside her was locked.

Later, she heard him open the door and come over and stand by the bed. He sat down with a sigh on the empty side of the bed and reached over and picked up a strand of her hair. Gently rubbing it between his fingers he said in a voice tight with emotion, "I want to stay married to you."

She turned and looked at him and felt tears welling in her eyes, "Me too, to you."

"I just...I just don't know how to let it go. I'm sorry..." his voice broke in a sob.

"Oh, John, no, no. *I'm* the one who's sorry." She pulled him down next to her and he buried his face in her neck. "I'm sorry, I'm sorry, I'm sorry," she whispered again and again, not knowing what else to say. Their tears mingled as she kissed his head. He cried out his pain and anguish against her breasts and she held him close feeling an exquisite wrenching that she was the cause of his great pain. She wiped the tears from his face, gently with her hand then slowly tilted his face, kissing his forehead, his eyes, his cheeks and then his mouth. He was so pliable, he was like a baby in her arms. She kissed him again and again, her tongue exploring his mouth, drawing his into her mouth. His hands pulled down the nightgown from her breasts and he touched her, then ducked his head until his mouth found her nipple.

Her tears fell on his head as she pressed him to her breast, "Oh, John, I love you I love you I love you I love you." She cried it over and over again, like a mantra, as though the repetition in itself would start the healing.

It had been so long since they were really intimate, not just having sex, that they were both ignited. His mouth drove her wild and she pulled him on top of her, guiding him into her, burying her face in his neck.

"John, John, you are my love. You are my only love."

He felt the heat as she wrapped her legs around him and moved in passionate rhythm with him and they knew that they were married again.

Chapter 23

Carol remembered the time she met William Wordsworth when she was a teenager. It was a weekend home from her freshman year of college and she was alone in the house, early on a Saturday evening. Her parents were out as were her older brother and sister.

In the living room of her parents house was a corner desk and a bookcase. It had a wide desktop, though no one ever used it as a desk. She sat on top of it, lotus fashion and opened her volume of *The Romantic Poets* to Wordsworth's *Ode on Intimations of Immortality* and began reading it out loud. She loved the resonance of Wordsworth's poetry, loved its accessibility and its tone. Because she was a closet performer, she loved exaggerating and dramatizing as she read. With anyone else at home, she never would have attempted this, but the privacy of an empty house encouraged it.

As she read verse after verse, she warmed up as an orator, got better at it, put more feeling into it. She held the book in one hand and gesticulated with the other toward the couch and chairs facing her. She pretended she had an audience, a future classroom perhaps, and with all her heart and love for these words, poured them forth with dramatic feeling.

Then, in a moment as swift as a heartbeat, she saw sitting on the couch facing her, an old man, white hair, white beard, watching her and sagely nodding his head, his large hand tapping on the arm of the sofa in metronomic precision to the Ode's cadence. Before anything like shock could register, she knew it was William Wordsworth, drawn here by her loving recitation. Her voice caught on itself and she stared open-mouthed.

"Go on" he seemed to say without actually speaking. Carol continued, more self-conscious now, but she also was aware that he was not so much interested in her as he was in the words she was reading. She interpreted this as vanity. She finished all eleven verses of the ode and before she could begin reciting another poem, he was gone, the couch empty as before.

She decided to tell no one of this experience. Who, after all would believe her? She was surprised at how little of a reaction she herself had, as though such apparitions happened to her everyday. It felt so natural and unthreatening, that she neither doubted nor questioned its validity. It was an experience that just happened.

Her fledgling philosophy on spiritual matters was that the intangible part of a person, never died. Something about us is immortal she always thought, some essence, some spiritual thing, maybe the Soul part of us, whatever that was. It made perfect sense to her that a poet such as Wordsworth was immortal because of his great poetry. And if he chose to visit a twentieth century admirer? Well, small task for one of the mighty immortals.

Chapter 24

Like DaVinci, Franklin's creative imagination was broad and free ranging, not limited to one field of endeavor. His insatiable curiosity was a facet of his fertile mind. Being pragmatic as well as inventive, he came up with things that people could use, that would improve things. Almost all of his inventions were practical and utilitarian.

Franklin was the inventor of bifocals; the "Franklin" stove; the lightning rod; the one armed-desk chair, (remember those from school days?); the copying press; the long arm for moving books in high shelves; a musical instrument, (the armonica); the four-sided ventilated lamp, (originally the old street lamps); a rocking chair that fanned as it rocked. He also invented the first flexible catheter. He designed the forerunner of the step ladder.

None, I repeat, none of his inventions were patented. He refused to do this, saying they were for the good of all. He gave them freely without expecting anything in return. (Surely this alone guarantees his immortality.)

He was the first postmaster general in America, designing and engineering the postal delivery system, and he founded the first lending library. He wrote the first syndicated column, founded the first magazine in America, and was the first to use cartoons in journalism. He formed the first fire department and the first police department, the first defense militia and the first fire insurance policy. He founded the first hospital and he started the American Philosophical Society (was its first president and remained so until his death).

He suggested daylight savings time, was the first to use oil to still unquiet waters, the first to discover the importance of frequent bathing, fresh air and ventilation.

He was the first to suggest a committee of nations to monitor world activities and he was the one who suggested foreign languages be taught in school. His scientific experiments with the water temperatures in the Gulf Stream were instrumental to its being charted.

Franklin was the first to design an experiment (using lightning) proving that electricity was a force of nature.

The first to receive an honorary doctorate from Harvard.

First to discover that white garments did not attract heat but black garments did.

He characterized lead poisoning.

Because of his inventions, he also invented the following words: battery, conductor, armature, brush, condense.

He had ideas for—but did not develop—the concept of a water bed, parachute, air conditioning, hearing aid.

He was the only American in our history to be given the power of Minister Plenipotentiary.

Someone said that George Washington was first in war, first in peace and first in the hearts of his countrymen, but Benjamin Franklin was first in everything else.

Chapter 25

Franklin was not outwardly a religious man. In fact, he was viewed as being rather indifferent to spiritual matters. Our famous Mr. Lawrence (among others) accused him of having no concern with the immortal soul. I believe I've already shown that Mr. Lawrence and Mr. Adams both had a limited ability to perceive anything beyond the edge of their nose, therefore I won't dwell further on their limitations.

The problem is, of course, that one can never know the state of another's soul. This is privileged information between Soul and God. One's outer religious affiliation or professed piety often does not accurately reflect one's inner state.

Franklin had little use for conventional religion; but then, religion doesn't always embrace spirituality. Religion can be social, cultural, political or expedient, but not necessarily spiritual. Because he did not overtly pay homage to organized religion does not mean he was not a profoundly spiritual man. In fact, he unequivocally was. His connection with the Almighty was direct, bypassing the human contingency of priestcraft, church, and other self-assigned intermediaries. He believed one's deepest spiritual beliefs were intensely personal and he shared them with no one in his lifetime. However, he shared them with me.

He summed up his religious credo in a letter to Madame Brillon in 1781 and again in a letter to the President of Yale near the end of his life. It was, he said, the belief he formed when he was young and found nothing convincing to alter it one way or the other. It was this:

"In every religion, beside the essential things, there are others, which are only forms and fashions, as a loaf of sugar may be wrapped in brown or white or blue paper, and tied with a string of flax or wool, red or yellow; but the sugar is always the essential thing. Now the essential principles of a good religion consist, it seems to me, of the following 5 articles, viz.:

1) That there is one God who created the Universe, and who governs it by His providence. 2) That He ought to be worshipped and served. 3) That the best service to God is doing good to men. 4) That the soul of man is immortal, and 5) That in a future life, if not in the present one, vice will be punished and virtue rewarded."

Maybe this seems simplistic to those who think a mind as brilliant as Franklin's should evolve a more sophisticated religious credo. I'm of two minds on this: he is either a simple man we try to make complex, or a complex man who yearns for simplicity. Either way, he kept his spiritual credo simple. He was not fond of dogma and doctrine, nor was he attracted to metaphysical thinking. He simply lived by, or lived simply, by his five-point credo.

Points one and two establish his monotheism and his belief that the Creator is supreme. Point three he literally lived: his entire life was spent in service to his fellow man. Four indicates his belief in the immortality of Soul, and five confirms his belief in reincarnation and karma. (Karma, of course, being the idea of cause and effect, or as he put it simply, 'What goes around, comes around.') Thus, he was aware that whatever he did in this life, he was responsible for and his actions would find reward or punishment in future lives.

We discussed the idea of 'responsibility' as a spiritual concept and which, after hearing his argument, I felt inclined to agree. He deplored the welfare state our country had fallen into, saying it took responsibility for one's self out of one's own hands.

"The government has no right to be involved in individual life as deeply as it is. Self-sufficiency is a mark of spiritual consciousness," he said. "When one expects a government agency to take care of one's corporal needs, one is shrugging off the very challenge that life has provided for one's spiritual growth. Each person is responsible for himself. To turn that very charge over

to another is to spiritually default on a gift. It is a crime for both the government and for the individual who cedes this right away from the self."

"What about those who can't take care of themselves?" I asked, thinking of the monthly donations John and I made to various charities.

"The sick of mind and body need help, I agree, and one must not begrudge it to the truly needy. But the able-bodied and able-minded who take these monies are leeches on every tax-paying citizen. There is always honest work for honest people. Unfortunately, those who accept the welfare state as their right, are not always honest people."

It seemed a rather strong indictment of our system, but I reminded myself that he helped formulate the principles on which this country was founded, and surely was entitled to comment on how it has progressed since its birth.

*"It was never intended that our Government have as much power as it does. Never. When we said a government of, by and for the people, we **meant** it, in the truest sense of the word democracy. People were to have been the primary source of political power; not the office created by the vote. What it has evolved to is deplorable."* He spoke sternly and with feeling. Then he shrugged and said with a cynical smile, *"But, that is progress, is it not?"*

In March of 1988 we got around to discussing his spiritual philosophy. I asked him, since nearly two hundred years had elapsed since his physical demise, had his spiritual thinking undergone any change?

"Indeed. But now, it is no longer 'credo,' I believe, but 'gnoscero,' I know. When one leaves this theater of existence," he waved his arms around my study, *"one is either affirmed in one's carefully held notions of the afterlife, or,"* and here his eyes twinkled merrily, *"one is greatly surprised that events are not at all what they surmised."*

"You rhymed", I said to him.

"I know."

"Religion," he continued, *"the way it manifests in these lower worlds, is primarily as a social function. It may or may not accurately reflect a person's spiritual beliefs, and sometimes it has nothing to do with God. Most people fail to make this distinction. Most people see religion as their statement of*

their deepest spiritual beliefs, yet often it is not even remotely associated with spirituality. Take Puritanism for example."

"No, you take it," I said.

We both laughed. He had this effect on me of cracking jokes in the midst of serious discussion.

"Puritanism," he continued still smiling at my joke, "was an attempt to regulate and confine the natural impulses in man for the sake of ordering society. Puritanism demanded that everyone be in agreement; that certain things were wrong and sinful and other things were right and just. To disobey these rules was a sign of heathenism, or worse, atheism. Puritanism repressed the imagination, which is a God-given gift. The worst thing a religion can do is to repress man's natural impulses."

"Meaning imagination?"

"That's one of them, yes. Puritanism's tool of control was guilt. I myself have no use for that," he deprecated, spreading his palms out and downward. "Guilt is a link in the negative chain that binds us to the negative world. When we live a life of responsibility we are no longer concerned with guilt. Guilt is imposed by the priestcraft or by the people, not by God. The feelings of guilt and shame are the greatest problem the Masters have in dealing with the human consciousness. These feelings create a wall of stone that blocks us from greater states of consciousness. The burden of guilt is oftentimes heavier than the vice that caused it."

I asked him about the common historical assumption that he had little concern with soul.

"Rubbish," he said with mild annoyance. "That's the sort of criticism that I paid little heed in my day. My friend, John Adams said it, slightly more eloquently than your audacious Mr. Lawrence, I might add."

"Not my Mr. Lawrence," I protested.

"Ours, then," he said and quickly continued.

"My relationship with The Divine Creator was and is very personal. I no more felt the need to render my beliefs public in my century than you do now. I did however, do what I was famous for; I diplomatically compromised by

maintaining an appearance of believing in religion, supporting and sustaining a church membership. I paid lip service and church dues."

"Politicians today do the same thing," I said. "Whoever is in office makes a big show about going to church, declaring a specific religion. I always doubt their sincerity."

"Some things in the human condition do not change. Hypocrisy is timeless," he shrugged.

When he said 'what I was famous for' it was in a self-deprecating, humorous tone that belied any pride or false modesty. I believe he truly was laughing at himself.

I was totally charmed by him. I well understood how the ladies of Paris felt about him. As a person, this man was irresistible.

I busied myself writing and he spoke no more that night except by a kind of silent impression that filled me with words as I wrote.

Carol read over that section of her manuscript and hesitated. She was losing her objectivity with this. This manuscript was nowhere near what the editor expected of her. She really needed to pre-warn them about this change of direction.

She began roughing out more of this chapter.

Can public figures, especially politicians, dare to give their true feelings about the subject of religion? It is required (then and now) that the public person outwardly conform to a traditional religion, and in the United States that means some form of Protestantism. Remember the big issue John Kennedy's Roman Catholicism was? The real feelings of these public men are not known, cannot be known, because society demands that they conform to what the masses accept or believe. True rebellion in religion is not permitted in public office. Individual and original thinking would not cut it in the White House. We want our leaders to be ordinary not extraordinary. We don't want innovation, we want sameness. We don't want anyone to rock the (religion) boat. Franklin knew and understood this two hundred years ago. Don't rock the boat. What indeed would be the point?

"The majority," he said, "are ill-inclined to believe they can be wrong."

*Carl Becker in **Dictionary of American Biographies** said: "Ben Franklin was…not wholly committed. Some thought remains uncommunicated, some penetrating observation is held in reserve."*

Franklin himself admits to the masks he wore to hide what he did not wish to show.

"I tell the secrets of my heart to only my heart," he said to me. "And I had to lock many secrets in my heart in that lifetime.

"To be a public servant, one had to conform to the prevailing image. Image was important, indeed, isn't that true today? Being a public servant, I was a man of image." He laughed heartily at his own words.

Many historians have commented on his many masks. He created the illusion that people wanted. He flirted (since that was expected of him); he joked, he bantered and bargained. He even may have let himself become a caricature. But was the true Franklin ever accessible to anyone?

"Is anyone ever what they appear to be?" he mused, reading over my shoulder. "Yes, yes, I played a game, but how could I have done otherwise? But you must note," he said firmly, tapping my computer with his forefinger, "that though it's true I maintained an image, I never, never compromised the ideals I committed to in my youth, when my origins and my destiny were shown to me.

"Remember the mirror. Always remember the mirror. I became a public mirror. Hypocrites always suspect hypocrisy in others and the greedy will always see greed in others. What Adams saw in me was but the echo of his own worse murmurings."

At another time I questioned him about his implied belief in reincarnation. Surely that theory was neither popular nor acceptable in his time?

"It always made sense to me. I thought even someone of pedestrian intelligence could comprehend that it couldn't be any other way. Do you really think the Divine Intelligence would make a soul only to destroy it after a few, insignificant years, one paltry lifetime? Do you not credit this Great Intelligence with greater planning? There are no mistakes, remember that. There are never any mistakes in the universe. All is going according to Divine Plan…right down to the chirping of a bird. We live to learn, then we live again and again and again. Anything else would be ludicrous."

His epitaph, (written by himself, of course) reflects his gentle self-deprecation, as well as his belief that he will be born again:

> *The body of*
> *B Franklin Printer,*
> *Like the Cover of an old Book*
> *Its Contents torn out*
> *And stript of its Lettering & Gilding*
> *Lies here, Food for Worms.*
> *But the Work shall not be lost;*
> *For it will (as he believ'd) appear once more,*
> *In a new and more elegant Edition*
> *Revised and corrected,*
> *By the Author."*

A thinker, like Franklin, who was a man ahead of his time in many areas, was a man out of his time in his spiritual beliefs as well.

God's purpose for men out of their time is to show others the way of the future.

Chapter 26

Carol was two years younger than her sister, Mary. The rivalry was between them for as far back as Carol could remember. Mary resented that she had to share a bedroom with her younger sister, and Carol resented her resentment. When they got into fights, Mary used her fists as weapons, hitting Carol where she could, pulling her hair, even biting if that was convenient. Often their mother had to intervene. Mary used whatever weapon was handy to wound Carol; nasty words when it was inconvenient to hit her. Carol, being smaller, often got beat up, but the cruel and unkind words hurt her more. Long after the sore arm stopped hurting from Mary's punch, the sting of the words stayed with her. She realized words hurt more than a punch and with this realization, things turned around. She had discovered the weapon that allowed her to be the victor.

Words. Because of her sister she had an early lesson in their power. Carol experimented with different words, tones and combinations that would elicit the most reaction from her sister. Initially she spewed venom and cruel words the way Mary did. Then she discovered sarcasm. It seemed, to Carol, a superior way of handling words and she cultivated it. Gradually she refined her weapon until, like an arrow, it left its bow with a sure aim and easily found its mark, wounding deeply. Carol was no longer defenseless.

One day Carol came home from her part-time job in a department store after school and told her mother, in amusement, that the Cuban boy who stocked shelves asked her to marry him. Since Carol was just sixteen and hardly knew the boy, she certainly didn't take him seriously and was amused, as she expected her mother to be. Mary, listening, said "It's because he knows you're a tramp."

Normally this kind of remark would have been an excuse to throw the first punch to Mary, but Carol merely looked at her frostily and said, "It takes one to know one." It was not a particularly clever comeback, mostly because their mother was there saying, "Now, girls, stop it." But something in Carol's delivery, a combination of scorn and amusement, infuriated Mary who would have continued the argument, except Carol turned and walked away.

Another time Mary called her a chameleon, thinking she had delivered an effective insult. Mary's face burned as Carol laughed, congratulating her on learning a new word. Carol couldn't be beat at this game. Mary came to dread arguing with Carol since her words were more vicious than anything Mary could think of. Carol was smarter and seemed to have more words in her arsenal than Mary.

It came to Carol one day like a rush of truth, that this antipathy between them was because Mary was jealous of her. It struck her with such simplicity that she wondered why she hadn't realized it before. Carol was prettier, her hair natural blond, her green eyes bright and alert. Mary's hair was mousy brown, her features plain. Carol was popular in school, made friends and straight As with equal ease. Mary had fewer friends and struggled to get Bs and Cs. Their brother Ron, one year older than Carol, obviously favored his younger sister. Mary resented that she was not the only girl in the family and she frequently said to Carol, "I hate you."

Their parents waited it out, hoping the bickering would stop with the teenage years. And in a way it did. As strong as words were as a weapon, Carol found as they got older, that it was just as effective to withhold words. She used silence to frustrate Mary. At least when Carol argued back, it was a response; but her silence was more contemptuous, since it told Mary she wasn't even worth fighting with.

It wasn't until they were adults that they reached a truce of sorts. Both married, Mary promptly had children and though they never became close, the fights of their adolescence ceased. Carol was the victor, they both knew, since any contest of wit and words would always be no contest. This never made Carol particularly happy. She wished her relationship with her sister could be better, but it wasn't. Later, in college, she learned what it meant to have a Pyrrhic victory.

Chapter 27

John and Carol were sitting in their screened-in porch, Sunday papers spread around them as they drank coffee and enjoyed the warm sun. Silently they passed finished sections to each other, commenting occasionally on something they read. Carol always started with the comics while John read the front page and then methodically read each section in order. After the comics and the magazine section, Carol randomly read whatever John passed to her. Occasionally they clipped coupons or cut out articles that might be useful in class or their research. This Sunday morning Carol was reclining on a lounge chair with a news section folded in front of her.

"Listen to this, John. This cop was trying to stop a robbery and it says quote, *he took a bullet in his head.* Jeez, can you believe that?"

"Um, you're surprised a cop got shot?"

"No, silly. I'm talking about the voice. He *took* a bullet is active. How does one *take* a bullet? Did he do it willingly for godsakes? *Received* would be more correct."

She continued reading and John smiled at her, amused.

"I don't think most people pay attention to language the way you do, honey."

"Of course they don't. It's pathetic how corrupted our language has become. Here's another good one. There was an accident on the turnpike last night and again I quote, it brought the turnpike to its knees.

Christ, what does that mean? Does a highway have knees? Does it have other body parts?"

"If the main purpose of language is to communicate, then it's working isn't it? I mean, the image of the turnpike being crippled is communicating something isn't it?"

She turned to him in mock disbelief. "Are you defending this rotten writing?"

"No. But the average person who reads the newspaper doesn't care if the metaphor is ridiculous as long as communication is served. The average reader understood that the turnpike was a traffic jam because of the accident."

"Then why not say the turnpike was closed because of an accident?"

"Because the journalist obviously felt it would be more interesting and creative to use the body metaphor."

"The journalist obviously knows squat about language. Reading the newspaper can be so annoying," she scowled turning back to the paper.

"Carol, you can't expect everyone to have your standards for language."

"It's not just my standards. It's their language too. People are so sloppy about language, the way it's spoken, the way it's written. These are the two main ways we communicate and so many have so little command of either method. It's really pathetic."

John knew she was teaching a slang and dialects course this semester and was especially sensitive to language abuses at the moment.

"And this, this is a real slop," Carol continued opening to the entertainment section. "Slang in journalism. How low can we go? Grrr."

John decided to refrain from being devil's advocate here. She could get on a roll about slang and he'd heard it all before.

"Here's the expression, 'the whole nine yards' and I'm not on the sports page. What does that mean exactly? What does that communicate to you?"

"You want me to answer, don't you?"

She recognized his resigned, martyr tone and she smiled at him, nudging him with her foot. "Nevermind."

They read in silence for awhile, Carol keeping her newspaper comments to herself while John got absorbed in the Book Review.

He noticed that she picked up a pencil and pad and was copying something from the newspaper. Her reading glasses were perched on her nose as she wrote.

"I'll probably regret asking, but what are you doing?"

She didn't look up, but kept writing. "Stuff for my class tomorrow. Samples of slang found in the Sunday paper. Wanna hear it?"

"Is it too late to retract my question?"

"Yes, you asked so here it is." She sat up and read from the pad.

"I was in the elevator and this perfect stranger got in and hit on me.

"So, I said to my brother, 'chill.'

"My mother always told me, don't air your dirty laundry in public.

"When I told the others, they cracked up."

"Carol honey, don't let this stuff get you bent out of shape. You're getting in a stew about nothing."

"Oh, you're cute, but thanks, that's two more."

"Do you know what I find ironic in all this?" he said putting the paper down.

"What?"

"On the one hand you are a purist who advocates flawless, slangless, English and is fastidious about it almost to the point of obsession."

"Yeah, so, what's the other hand?"

"This is best illustrated," he said getting up and going inside the house. She waited perplexed.

He returned and handed her a note.

"*This* is the other hand."

She recognized it was a note she wrote to him yesterday. *J, pleez pik up the dry cleaning and if u hav a chance, take my car thru the car washr. thanx luv.*

"What's your point?" she asked keeping a straight face. "There's absolutely no slang in this note."

He raised his eyebrows in mock surprise. "This looks like it was written by a semi-literate."

"I beg your pardon, but are you objecting to the phonetic spelling?"

"Yes, quite. What was *your* point?"

She looked at the note. "My *point* was to eliminate a few letters thereby making it faster to write. Some words have so many useless letters. Take 'through', for example. The o, g and h are silent, so why not eliminate them? Words like this are throwbacks to Old English when they were pronounced. We've changed the pronunciation, why not adjust the spelling accordingly? I've never been against modernization, you know."

"Is this some new theory you've evolved? I don't recall you ever being a proponent of phonetic spelling."

"It's the law of economy. Why waste time writing out all those letters that are silent anyway? Besides, think how it would simplify learning the language. Do you know that English is one of the hardest languages in the world to learn? Of course you know that, but foreigners who try to learn English are forever confused by our vagaries, our slang, our spellings and our duplicitous meanings. *There, their, they're.* Why do we have to have the same sound, different spellings, different meanings? Or take a word like island. What the hell good is the s except to confuse people. Salmon. Throw out the l. Throw it the l out, I say." She giggled at her own funny.

"Or how about new, knew, the c and k sounds, the s and c sounds, and so on? English is a monstrously hard language to learn. Phonetics would simplify and clarify."

"This is new, isn't it?"

"Well, I guess so. It just suddenly made sense."

He thought for a moment, his forehead knitting in concentration.

"Didn't Benjamin Franklin propose a phonetic alphabet? Wasn't that one of his pet projects?"

"Yes."

"And didn't he find it impossible to implement, nevermind that he couldn't get anyone to agree with him?"

"I think it was something like that, why?"

"Just curious that you're doing this research on him and now you're taking up his causes."

"Oh, John, I'm not taking up his cause. Just because I use phonetics in a note to you doesn't mean I'm going to advocate it in my classes or anything."

He chuckled. "I can see it now. And they thought your Chaucer paper made a stink. You'd certainly raise some eyebrows with a phonetic alphabet theory."

"Well, now you're tempting me. If I can raise eyebrows or irritate some authority, maybe I should go for it." She smiled at him mischievously.

"Why did Franklin like phonetics?"

"I think because he believed English was a hard language to learn and our traditional spellings made it harder. He thought phonetics would simplify and clarify."

He looked at her thoughtfully.

Later when Carol was in her study working on her notes for her slang class, she heard a distinct sentence in her head: *Slang is like weeds, you know; you pull one out and ten more will replace it.* It was the soft voice of Ben.

"So I shouldn't fight it?" she said aloud.

"No. Only if the struggle amuses you. You can never hope to win."

"It's hard to make changes, isn't it?"

"Change is not easily accomplished," he agreed. "Most people resist it. When there are changes to be made in the universe, the Great Intelligence that runs the universe does it over time, so gradual that we fail to notice...like the Grand Canyon for example. That didn't appear overnight. Cataclysmic changes can devastate; gradual change is acceptable."

"But we do have cataclysmic changes in the world."

"Yes. Sometimes the world needs devastation, and when it does the Great Intelligence supplies it."

"This Great Intelligence...do you mean God?"

"God, Spirit, Buddha, Jehovah. Call it what you will. I call it the Great Intelligence as a philosophical metaphor. Too many people are attached to the idea of a grandfatherly, human- type God. It's all they can relate to."

"And the truth is?"

"The truth is, God is more like an Ocean...an ocean of love and mercy. Words can only describe IT lamely." His voice trailed off.

"What does God have to do with language?" she asked bringing the subject back to what she was working on.

"In a way, God has everything to do with language. Who do you think invented it?"

She considered the question seriously, not seeing the twinkle in his eye.

"Language evolved through need...and circumstances," she recited academically. "You know, the wheel was invented, so we needed a word to describe it; just so with all inventions, right up to our computers, likewise."

"If you only knew how many eons it took for language to catch on in the human consciousness."   .

"My theory is wrong?"

"Not wrong," he said diplomatically, "but very surface."

She blushed at the criticism. "Studies of language show that it evolved from hand gestures to grunts to refined grunts to words. And that finally, at the birth of language, humanness too, took a leap forward, forever separating us from animals."

"In essence, that's quite true," he replied. "While standing upright was our first physical separation from the animal kingdom, language, certainly, is what allowed us to rise above them."

"And you're saying God had a direct hand in this?"

"God has always, the help of masters...beings who have attained complete and consciousness awareness of God...who work for the Great Intelligence in the lower worlds. It is these beings, these spiritual masters who work directly with the human consciousness on the human level. They work tirelessly and eternally to uplift the consciousness. The evolution of language was a tremendous creative effort that took a vast period of time to bring about."

"I appreciate it," she said, awed.

He looked at her and nodded. "Gratitude is good."

"Then this," she lifted her class notes on slang, "this deterioration of language is..."

"Is reflective of, unfortunately, general deterioration in the human condition." She detected a note of sadness in his voice.

"Why do I bother with this then?"

"You've got to do something while you're here."

She looked at him quickly and saw that he was smiling.

"Oh, Ben," she smiled too. "You're always making jokes."

"Despite that, there is a purpose for your love of language. There's a purpose for every single thing under the sun. Because of your love for language, you get many of the life experiences that you need."

She though wryly of her affair with the English linguist.

"Yes, even that," Ben said watching her face.

She looked up guiltily. "You know about *that*?"

"Carol, Carol, don't you understand? I know *everything* about you just as you know everything about me."

But I don't know everything she started to say as his arms crossed his chest and he slowly dissolved into the ethers. She felt the emptiness of the room and she stared for a moment at the space he had occupied. Then with a sigh she turned to her desk and her class notes on slang and dialects.

Chapter 28

"John, how do you feel about taking a trip to Connecticut with me?

"Pourquoi?"

"I want to look at some of the Franklin papers at Yale. Do you want to go with me?"

"When?"

"May? As soon as classes are over. We could drive out, maybe spend a week?"

"I guess so. I'm sure I can find something to do at Yale while you're reading Ben's love letters."

"He didn't write love letters," she said irritably.

"I was only joking. Why are you being so sensitive about this?"

"Look, do you want to go or shall I go alone? I'm going to make an appointment for the last week in May."

"I'll go with you...unless you'd rather go alone."

"If I go alone, I'll fly. If you go, we'll drive, make a little vacation out of it."

"I think we could both use a vacation."

*   *   *

They settled in a hotel not far from the Yale campus and Carol went to the library to examine the Franklin papers. The editors of the

Franklin collection were very helpful, giving her the letters and docu-
ments she wished to examine. She sat in a small room with a pencil and
a notebook and read, occasionally making writing notes on what she was
reading. She felt privileged to be handling these rare and valuable items.
She touched the fragile letters, some over two hundred years old and felt
awe as she looked at Franklin's neat handwriting. He was so articulate,
his writing so legible. Like other areas of his life, his penmanship was
ordered and precise.

She worked through the first morning then met John for lunch. He'd
been exploring the library as well, having made contact with another
medieval scholar and was planning to meet with him that afternoon.

"What do you think of this?" she asked, playfully taking his hand as
they left the campus. "All these trees, all this austere history at this vener-
able institution?"

"Impressive. But I'm happy with Bodley. Our campus is pretty, too."

"Yeah, but this is Yale, John."

"What are you finding with old Ben?"

"Nothing unexpected. I didn't expect to find the unexpected, though.
There's just so much that hasn't even been published, they tell me it may
take another twenty years before all of his writings are published. Franklin
corresponded with over four thousand people in his lifetime. Imagine."

"How did he have time to do anything else but write letters?"

"He's amazing."

"You mean, *was* amazing."

Carol caught herself and looked at him quickly. Soon she'd have to level
with him about what was going on; so far she justified her reluctance to
do so by saying it was not the right time. If she was going to put herself
on the firing line, John had to know about it in advance.

"The woman at the library told me about a deli not too far where we
can get a good lunch. We turn here, I think she said."

Now that a lot of the students had gone for the summer, New Haven
was just an ordinary town, none too attractive, Carol thought. The

campus was unique, but the town was just a town. For a moment she missed Numen and the comfortable familiarity of *her* town.

She spent the rest of the afternoon in the library reading unpublished material, losing track of time until she glanced at her watch and realized it was nearly seven p.m. Carol was surprised that she'd been sitting for five hours straight.

Once during the afternoon, she felt the distinct presence of Ben and almost unconsciously started talking to him. She caught herself quickly as a librarian glanced at her.

"Telepathy works just as well," he whispered and she giggled, pretending to find something amusing in the letter she was reading.

"I'm worried about how the manuscript is shaping up," she confided to him silently. "It's not what I've been hired to write and I don't think they'll like what I've written."

"Hmmm," he seemed to be rubbing his chin, pondering this information. "I think this will turn out to be exactly what you were hired to write...if you consider that I am the one who did the hiring."

She closed her eyes a moment and tried to ascertain if he were serious. He seemed to have left, so she continued reading.

She spent three days examining the Franklin collection, then she and John set off for the drive home. They had a leisurely drive, stopping to visit historic places between Connecticut and Illinois. Carol worked on her notes as John drove and occasionally took a turn at the wheel to give him a rest. As she drove she tried to understand what was the point of the trip to Yale. She learned very little new information; at least what was pertinent to her subject, yet it had seemed important to her to make the trip. She mused about Franklin as the miles sped away.

When they'd been back home a few days, she wrote the introduction to her book which she knew was crucial to her thesis. She had to explain, somehow, not only the manuscript content, but the metaphysical approach she'd taken. Though she tried to be objective and thorough in the explanation, she also knew she needed to be honest. It was the reception of this honesty that concerned her. It sounded so far out, even to her, and it was this aspect that she knew would give her trouble. She was ready for another viewpoint on this.

"How busy are you right now?" she asked John when he came home from work.

"Middling. Why, whatcha need?"

"I'd like you to read part of the manuscript and give me some feedback."

"Sure, I'd love to. I was wondering when I'd get a chance."

She smiled sardonically. "I tell you what, I'll go out and get your favorite Chinese meal while you read this." She handed him the chapter. "Be back in a bit."

Chapter 29

The Truth About Benjamin Franklin
Introduction

*First of all, let me declaim that I have **not** had a lifelong fascination with Benjamin Franklin. So often, "lifelong fascination" is the justification for a book on the subject. In fact, I hardly had an interest in him at all until this past year. My knowledge of him was limited to that which everyone else probably has; that is, he invented a lot of things, made up a lot of pithy proverbs, was one of the founding fathers of our country, lived in Philadelphia, etc. etc.*

In late 1987, references to Franklin began to appear in my life. I picked up a magazine and saw a picture of him; I went to a restaurant and found it had a Revolutionary War theme and I was at the Ben Franklin table; a friend mentioned his new Franklin stove; a student's paper mentioned his visit to the Franklin museum in Philadelphia; an anecdote about him in a lecture I attended; in Trivial Pursuit I got all the Ben Franklin questions, and so it went.

None of these incidents in themselves would have meant a thing. It was only the insistent repetition that finally caught my attention. Was it just coincidence or was something else going on? Is it true, as some believe, that there really are no coincidences in life? I wondered what it could mean.

When one asks a question, can the answer be far behind?

Within a week of wondering this, I was contacted by Marietta Davison of Virago Press proposing a book idea. Though the topic wasn't fully formulated, the general plan was to target the sexist attitudes of the founding fathers. The most significant coincidence yet!

*It's been my experience that Life (please note the capital L which denotes personification); always provides us with exactly what we need to grow. Nevermind that we most often miss these opportunities; nevermind that we don't even **like** most of them. Life will continue to do its job and put before us our plate of experiences.*

Therefore, having been prepared by the potpourri of Ben Franklin references, I recognized this was something that was ineluctably mine, and for whatever unknown reason, I was to write a book on Ben Franklin.

Since Virago is somewhat of a feminist press, the basic, general theme of the book was to show how sexism was part of the founding fathers' philosophy on which our country was formed.

Eighteenth century men may have been Reasonable men but that doesn't mean they were necessarily Enlightened about the inequalities that existed between the sexes. Hence, it seemed an easy task to research the men and the times for sexism. I accepted the assignment.

Unsure of the exact trajectory I wanted my arrow to take, (for I was sure it would be an arrow), I began reading, hoping a specific direction would come to me. So, one day I'm happily reading Flannery O'Connor; the next I'm doing research on Benjamin Franklin, books and note cards spread out, wondering what I'm looking for.

Now I have to jump to a seemingly unrelated subject: dreams, and ask your patience to follow me through a brief discourse here, assuring you that it is indeed connected to the subject.

I've always been a dreamer, both figuratively and literally, but here I'm talking about the literal kind of dreams: those scenes that occur when we sleep. They were always part of my life, but their meanings eluded me. I doubted their importance, sloughing them off by saying, "It's just a dream."

But part of me knew better. Dreams are too pervasive in the human consciousness to be meaningless. I've read books on dreams by psychics and psychologists (who else writes about dreams?) searching for the clue that would unravel the mystery of the dream state. Bits and pieces of the many theories of dreams seemed to contain elements of truth, but none totally satisfied me.

Eventually, what evolved for me, and what continues to evolve, is an understanding of what the dream state actually is, what its importance is and how it relates to our waking life.

From ancient times when rulers engaged prophets to interpret their dreams, to Jung and Freud and present day, dreams fascinate and perplex. We assume they mean something, but what? I will simplify here to say that Dreams (personified also) provide us with opportunities to learn valuable lessons in life, by giving us actual, real experiences in a non-physical world. Did you get that? I said Actual, Real Experiences.

Now back to Ben Franklin and subject book. OK, so I'm reading, vaguely heading in the direction of making mincemeat of him, for no special reason other than that was the assignment. I had several dreams about him. Now, you might say this is perfectly normal since my waking hours are spent thinking about him. But these dreams were not random as dreams often are. They showed me aspects of Franklin that I could not have gleaned from a history book…a private conversation with George Washington, one with Marie Antoinette…and my own observations which differed slightly from the books I've read.

Curious, and interesting, and it started me thinking.

*Then, one night I went to sleep and, (there is no other way to say it), he **appeared** in my dream; alive, almost tangible and so real I felt I was there with him, not dreaming at all. He outlined the book he wanted me to write. Incredibly, I found myself agreeing with him.*

*The next day, I was back to the dream books trying to understand these experiences. The feeling of **reality** in what happened was too much to ignore. Dream books led me to metaphysical books which led to spiritual books which led to some understanding of dreams. I've come to regard certain dream theory as Truth.*

My questioning started with basics: If the body is asleep and the mind is asleep (psychics and scientists agree on that), then WHO, or more accurately, WHAT part of me is having the dream experience? I knew it was ME that had the dream, but body and mind being unconscious, what part was awake in the dream? This thing we've called "soul", could that be the part that is awake at night? And if it is, WHAT is it?

*I found books that dealt with this subject and I got excited, for I **knew** I was on the right track. If you've ever done research on any subject, you know there is a feeling when you've found something valuable…that Eureka! feeling. You just **know**. Here's a short distillation of some of what I learned:*

*We have more than one body. This physical self we all have, the flesh, blood, bones, organs, etc. is one. It's the body we know and many people think is the total. But there's also a mental body: our thoughts, ideas, intellect. Our emotional, feeling body is another. Our memory of things from past lives is a fourth body. But the most important one, the one that connects all these bodies and oversees all the functions of each body is the Soul body; for this is what we are. Soul is **who we are**. This is the essence, the highest part of us. **We are Soul** and the other parts of us are facets of our true self, all connected and all necessary to function in this world.*

All of these bodies use or work through or express themselves through the physical body, since we are living in a physical world. In order to live here, this outer covering, the physical body is necessary. When we cease to live in the physical world, this body is dropped or "dies" and we use only the other four bodies; they do NOT die. Thus, dreaming is dropping the physical body for the time that we sleep, and having experiences in our non-physical bodies in the interior worlds.

In the dream state, or non-physical world there is no matter, energy, space or time. You can be anywhere just by being there. If that sounds confusing, think of a dream in which you are walking on a street in your hometown and the next instant you're swimming in the surf of Hawaii. We all know that dreams are not logical in the same way that we demand logic in the physical world. Nor are they necessarily chronological. Things occur in dreams that wouldn't be possible in the physical, waking world. We've come to accept the illogic of the dream state, but do we understand it?

Once I understood that my "other" bodies had experiences much as my waking, physical life did, I began to look at those experiences with a new appreciation for the subtleties of this larger force that was operating in the universe. There had to be a higher power, larger force, divine plan, call it what you will. Nothing short of that made any sense to me. Calling it God somehow always embarrassed me; that attempt to personalize something that seemed so remote and impersonal. I call this force "Spirit"...the invisible, the benign, possibly divine, guiding arm of the positive force that regulates the worlds we live in.

Accepting Spirit as the regulator or maker of my dream state, opened me to incredible dream experiences, the gift of recall, lucid dreaming, and, most important, an awareness of the reality of dreams.

Since there is no matter, energy, space or time in the "inner" or non-physical worlds, it is possible to get on the "time track," that is, a train-like thought form which moves us to the past or to the present, as we understand them, and experience slices of life from those times. It is also possible for communication to occur between compatriot Souls, for want of another way to describe that.

This is what occurred one night, about two months after my attention was first drawn to Benjamin Franklin.

Basically what he conveyed was that he was a little dismayed about the reputation history had given him concerning his behavior towards women. A popular belief is that he was lecherous, a "dirty old man", a womanizer, especially in his later years. This image of him is one that I, too, vaguely had, without knowing any facts. This upset him, for he felt it was untrue and unfair. He asked if I would try to correct this.

Because of my experiences with him, I was able to see that his fondness for women was neither a weakness nor pure lust, but more of a romantic, chivalric attitude, a genuine liking of women, an understanding of them and a preference for their company. The main attraction wasn't sexual; but rather he loved and recognized women's strength, their intuitiveness, their tenderness. He was a champion for their rights. In short, he was a feminist.

For me, a staunch and outspoken feminist, to accept this explanation of his sexual behavior without doubt, was an affirmation that one Soul communicating with another in the inner planes, can only communicate truth. Beyond the mental, physical and emotional planes it is impossible for lies to exist, for there is no duality on the Soul Plane. Soul, without the encumbrances of its other bodies is pure and seeks only truth.

When I first found myself back in the 18th century in the company of this great man, he was sitting conversing with George Washington, and so fascinated was I with Franklin that I scarcely gave Washington a glance. My first observation, after I got over my awe at being there, was that he was taller than I supposed, his nostrils had more of a flair than pictures indicate, and he wasn't as rotund as he was in our modern depictions of him. Washington said very little, but listened, charmed and amused, to Franklin's witty monologue. I sat there, invisible, and so impressed with the humorous way he spoke, the lightness and the gentle teasing manner he entertained with his clever conversation. This confirmed the historical accounts of his sense of humor.

In another dream, he stood behind Marie Antoinette as she sat at a mirror (applying makeup?) No words were spoken, and though he appeared courtly towards her, I sensed an amused, almost sardonic attitude toward her. The fact that she closely studied her face in the mirror while he looked on indicated her vanity; that she sat while he stood, almost subservient behind her, conveyed her feeling of superiority; that she allowed him there while she was preening was patronizing. Though this was only my interpretation of the dream, (but then, it was my dream), these attitudes (hers and his) have, in fact, been verified in my research.

My third dream experience with him took place in a large room, with large tables on which were spread papers of a manuscript. He indicated these were mine, I was to write a book about him and he would show me the direction it was to take.

Since that time, the dreams with him have been numerous. We've had conversations, shared jokes, and discussed dreams, philosophy, spirituality, modern politics, science and love. He is as urbane, witty, sincere and intelligent as history portrays him. He is nearly as alive to me as any friend I have.

He has guided the writing of this book in ways I never could have imagined a year ago.

On a practical level, (for my association with him has emphasized that quality), this has taught me a new way to enhance and expand my research. Never more will I be limited to the walls of a library to explore any subject. As a man in his time, he never knew any frontiers. It was that quality that enabled him to accomplish the enormous and wide-ranging list of achievements he accrued in one lifetime. From him I've learned that none of us...not me, not you, not anyone...now or at any time, need ever accept any frontier that tries to limit the free and probing human spirit.

Carol T. Byrd,
Numen, Illinois
October, 1988

John sat in his chair, the pages on his lap and stared at the space in front of him. He heard her car pull into the driveway and the front door open and close. He heard her in the kitchen, getting plates and utensils out, and then her footsteps coming to his study.

"Dinner's ready, thanks to Chang. Are you hungry?" she opened the door smiling at him. He stared at her and she saw the look on his face. She glanced at the papers in his lap.

"So, you didn't like it? Or does that look mean you're in awe of my writing ability?"

"You can't be serious about this?"

"Of course I'm serious."

He looked at her and saw the wariness in her eyes.

"Carol where are you going with this? This introduction doesn't promise scholarship, it's like new age mumbo jumbo. I can't believe you're serious. If this is your premise, you'll never get this published. Has anyone else seen this?"

"Jeez, don't beat around the bush or anything...just come right out and say you don't like it." She took the pages from him.

"Honey, I'm concerned. This isn't like you at all. What are you doing?"

"I thought my introduction made it pretty clear what I'm doing," she said slowly. She was counting on John to understand and support her in this, the way he always had. She didn't expect this reaction.

"You're saying you've had...*intercourse* with Benjamin Franklin."

"Oh, John, you're probably the only person in the 20th century who would still use that word to mean conversation."

"All right then, you've had communication with him?"

"That's what I said, didn't I? I mean, I wrote it pretty much as it happened."

"But Carol, that's impossible."

"It's not impossible, John, it happened."

He stared at her and she met his gaze unwavering. Finally he shook his head slowly.

"They'll cream you on this one, babe. This isn't like attacking Chaucer...this is academic suicide."

She allowed herself a small smile.

"What can I say? It's the truth. It seemed incredible to me at first too, but..." her voice trailed off and she shrugged. "Let's go eat. The lo mien is getting cold."

He walked behind her to the kitchen and put his hands on her shoulders. "Don't worry, honey, we'll get the best doctors, we'll find a cure for you, we'll beat this together."

She started laughing as she tossed his hands off her shoulders. She turned around and threw herself in his arms, holding him tightly.

"I don't know what I'd do without you, John Byrd."

He kissed the top of her head. "If you think that'll get you my share of the shrimp toast, forget it."

She tilted her head back to look at him. "I love you."

Chapter 30

The editor removed her glasses and set them on top of the manuscript and glanced away from Carol almost as though she were embarrassed.

"Professor Byrd, um, I'm not sure what to say here." She looked again at the manuscript laying on her desk and frowned. "This isn't quite..."

"I know it isn't 'quite'" Carol said quickly, relieving some of the tension. "I'll be the first to admit that this is definitely a dramatic departure from what you expected from me." She smiled. "Nonetheless, I think this is important to publish." She waited, trying to appear unconcerned.

"You're going to stand by this," she tapped the pages, "as is? You don't want to reconsider and rewrite this?"

"I don't think so. It's pretty straightforward. I'm not concerned with my academic reputation—I do have tenure fortunately", she joked. "My concern is, will you publish this or do I have to look elsewhere?"

"Professor Byrd, to be honest, I don't think I can use this as part of the series we originally designed and asked you to write. It just *isn't* what we had in mind. Instead of exposing patriarchal prejudices in the founding fathers, you're *defending* him. I confess I'm curious. Why?"

Carol shifted in her seat, uncomfortable explaining a philosophical position that was so new to her.

"Let's just say this whole thesis is a supposition. Suppose Ben Franklin could speak today and defend himself from the charges leveled against him? This might be what he would say. Look at this as a work of imagination."

The editor looked relieved. "Oh, you mean, you just *imagined* what he would say to the charges?"

Carol smiled and shrugged, raising her eyebrows as if to say, sure, why not.

"That does put it in a different light. Except, it's still not quite what we wanted. Perhaps you could call it a novel?"

"Look at it this way," Carol tried another angle. "What you would be doing would be daring...ground breaking. If you cling to only the traditional interpretation of feminist viewpoints, you fall into the same trap any discipline falls into by not being willing and open to change. This could be a cutting edge development in criticism, the expanded, new age, feminist viewpoint. Virago Press would be the avant garde, the leader of this. This is an opportunity to break molds, expand the parameters of an approach to criticism that is limiting."

The editor looked impressed, but not entirely persuaded.

Carol saw her advantage and pressed on. "You could be walking away from an opportunity for unlimited free advertising. Just suppose this does pick up a buzz. If it generates a lot of controversy...or at least attention, well, it could be a big deal for Virago Press."

"I'll have to clear this with the chief editor. It may require a board meeting to OK it. I'm sorry, Professor Byrd, it's just too...well it's more than controversial, it's unbelievable." She seemed to settle on that word though she was thinking another.

Carol picked up her brief case and purse. "OK, I'll wait to hear from you. I will totally understand if you decide against publishing this. On the other hand," she smiled sweetly, "I think you'd be making a mistake." She stood up to leave.

The editor likewise stood, smiled, and held out her hand. "I'm not saying we won't; I'm just saying we need to think about this one. It's different."

*   *   *

"Well, that's not quite as bad as I expected." John said later as they sat having tea on their porch. "Though I doubt they'll publish it."

"What? You have no faith in my outrageousness? I think it'll fly. They'd be foolish not to publish something like this, that will undoubtedly create a stir, in our limited circle, of course."

"I think they have a credibility thing to consider. If they go out on this limb with this type of book, what are they opening themselves to? Not only the criticism, but a loss of confidence in their respectable reputation as a bastion of feminist reliability. It's their risk as much as yours."

"I suppose." She didn't appear too concerned.

"What will you do if they say no?"

"Look for another publisher I think. I mean, why not?"

*   *   *

Later that night while she slept, Ben came again and took her to the conference room where they'd originally discussed the book. As before, she seemed to float in a sea of white light as they sat at the table. She started to tell him the possibility that the editor would not accept the book, and it may not get published. He waved her concerns away.

"Do you think I would have brought you this far without a publisher? Don't fret, that's finished."

"Finished? It isn't a book yet."

He smiled and gestured to a shelf where she saw a book with her name on it. She read the title *The Truth About Benjamin Franklin*. It was a dark blue cover with a gold patterned trim. Astonished, she looked at him but he just smiled.

"I told you once before, things happen here first. Time to move on. Let's get to the matter at hand."

It was only then that she noticed papers and note cards spread out on the table and somehow knew they were hers. She picked up a card and though it appeared to be in that strange hieroglyphics, she got an impression of the 19th century Romantic movement in poetry. She looked at Franklin, perplexed.

"This isn't my field."

He smiled gently, stroking his chin, "Your field?" Then he laughed delightfully. "Carol, Carol, *You* are your field. Haven't you learned that yet? This is all about getting to know *you*." His eyes looked deeply into hers and she was caught in a timeless moment where she felt there was something to comprehend and that his intense gaze was trying to communicate.

"There's someone I'd like you to meet" he said finally, softly, turning slightly away from her towards a doorway that appeared just as he looked that way. "Junkets, are you there?"

"Am indeed, guv." Carol saw a young man with an unruly mop of reddish-brown hair enter. His large eyes went to hers instantly and she noticed they were a hazel reflection of her own. He was short, around five feet she guessed, and he had a thick cockney accent. She knew in a flash this was John Keats; knew this like a jolt of recognition, though she didn't know how she knew this.

Franklin looked at him fondly and put his hand on Keats' shoulder.

"Junkets will cooperate with you fully on this next, mutual project." Franklin watched Carol carefully and saw the struggle to comprehend the connection and then he saw a question flicker in her eyes followed by an unbelieving comprehension.

Keats sat down in a chair across from her and toyed idly with a pencil that was on the table. His lustrous, clear eyes looked at Carol and she sensed shyness as well as an amused knowing. His plain face was enlivened by the humor that seemed to lurk just below the surface of his eyes.

He was watching her carefully as she looked towards Ben, who was rapidly fading; a vision of white light that disappeared even as she watched. She looked around and found she was alone with John Keats.

"Shall we begin?" he asked smiling.

the end

About the Author

Joyce G. Snyder studied at Southern Illinois University, Carbondale, before earning a BA *cum laude* from Douglass College in New Jersey. She also studied British Literature, Economics and History at Oxford University in England, and received a Master's degree in English from Rutgers University.

Her poems have been published in the literary journals, *Monmouth Review* and *I.E.* among others. She has written book reviews, essays, articles and poetry for holistic and spiritual magazines and newsletters. She is a former creative writing teacher and editor.

A life-long fascination with dreams and reincarnation led to the pursuit of a spiritual life that studies and explores these interests. She conducts workshops on dreams, past lives, karma and related subjects. At annual ECKANKAR international writers' conferences, she facilitates workshops on writing topics and how writing is a tool in one's spiritual quest.

She lives in New Jersey at the shore.

Bibliography

Barbour, Brian, M., "Franklin, Lawrence and Tradition," *Benjamin Franklin, A Collection of Critical Essays*. New Jersey: Prentice-Hall, 1979.

Becker, Carl, *The Examined Self: Benjamin Franklin, Henry Adams, Henry James*. Princeton: Princeton University Press, 1964.

_____ "Franklin's Character" *Benjamin Franklin, A Collection of Critical Essays*. New Jersey: Prentice-Hall, 1979.

Bowen, Catherine Drinker, *The Most Dangerous Man in America, Scenes from the Life of Benjamin Franklin*. Boston: Little, Brown, 1974.

Clark, Ronald W., *Benjamin Franklin, A Biography*. New York: Random House, 1983.

Lawrence, D.H., "Benjamin Franklin," *Benjamin Franklin, A Collection of Critical Essays*. New Jersey: Prentice-Hall, 1979.

Lopez, Claude-Anne, *Mon Cher Papa, Franklin and the Ladies of Paris*. New Haven: Yale University Press, 1966.

_____ and Herbert, Eugenia, *The Private Franklin, The Man and his Family.* New York: W.W. Norton, 1975.

Randall, Willard, *A Little Revenge.* Boston: Little, Brown, 1984.

Smith, Page, *John Adams.* New York: Doubleday, 1962.

Van Doren, Carl, *Benjamin Franklin, A Biography.* New York: Bramhall House, 1938.

Ward, John W., "Who was Benjamin Franklin?" *The American Scholar, XXXII* (Autumn, 1963), 541-53.

_____ "Benjamin Franklin: The Making of an American Character," *Benjamin Franklin, A Collection of Critical Essays.* New Jersey: Prentice-Hall, 1979.

Wright, Esmond, *Franklin of Philadelphia.* Cambridge, Mass: Belknap Press of Harvard, 1986.

Printed in the United States
814800003B